The Last Meal

Robert Middlet

CONTENTS

CHAPTER 1

T he holiday home was quaint. That was the only way to describe it.

I wondered how much Jack had paid for the rental, but I knew that he would never in a million years confide in me about that. Finances were just never discussed in our household. In fact, there was no joint account. Jack and I had separate VISAs. Every month, he'd deposit a certain amount of money into my account. That was just the way it was, the way it had always been over the ten years of our marriage.

"Holly arrived here yesterday. Sofia? Earth to Sofee."

Jack's gruff voice pulled me out of my thoughts, back to Earth, and back into his Lexus.

I snapped my head in his direction, pulling off my Ray-Bans and rubbing my eyes. "That's good. I can't be bothered to start dusting right now."

Holly Carter had been our maid – and my confidante – for years now. In fact, when I married Jack, I married her as part of the bargain. She was forty-five, five years older than my husband, plump, and always had a smile on her wrinkled face. She was a godsend and one of the few friends I had.

"The housewife that can't clean," Jack quipped, forcing some lightness into his voice. He pushed open the door and got out, stretching after our two-hour drive from London into The Comptons.

I stared after him, eyes concrete. Despite his forced joking tone, I knew how much it irked Jack that I couldn't so much as polish a marble floor. But it irked me that he had never taken me seriously when it came to my job. After the first two months of our marriage, he'd convinced me to quit my job at the hospital. That job had been my saving grace and he...took it from me.

"You coming out?" he demanded.

I squeezed my eyes shut. "Yes. I'm coming out."

Early twilight, after dinner, was the best time to do it.

Jack took such an amazingly long time to come to bed, and this "vacation" was no exception. I had seen that, aside from sending Holly up early, he'd taken the liberty of sending some of his office work up as well, and he was now shut in the study in the next room.

Old habits die pretty fucking hard, I thought bitterly, discarding the Agent Provocateur lingerie I'd bought specifically for our first night in The Comptons.

Naked, I stood in front of the mirror, analysing my body. Maybe I just wasn't attractive anymore. Maybe Jack preferred one of the young, bouncy interns at his law firm. Hell, maybe he was boinking her on the regular. Maybe she got the honour of blowing him on weekdays.

At my age, my body wasn't exactly runway-eligible, but it wasn't a horror show. Cupping my breasts in both hands, I figured perhaps they could've been a little less saggy. And that lone stretch mark on my right boob? It was like a silent accusation: Your boobs are too big for your ageing body, missy. Too large, and too saggy. What are you, fifty?

I glanced at the closed bedroom door, then turned my gaze back to the mirror. If Jack wasn't going to make me feel good about myself, well, then I just had to do the job myself.

Eyes trained on my reflection, I let my fingers trail down my stomach, slowly tickling over my navel, and into the soft mound of curls I kept for Jack, whenever he dared to venture down there – which was...never.

I don't know how long I spent trying to come – toying with my clít, rubbing my palm against it, heck, even begging my pus$y to feel something – but it sure as hell didn't work.

Damn Jack.

He'd even taken the pleasure of pleasure away from me.

CHAPTER 2

"Sofia?"

I blinked, squinting in the startling light. Jack had flicked all the bedroom lights on and was currently hovering above me, a scowl on his face.

"What time is it?" I croaked as I sat up, although I could already tell that it was an ungodly hour.

"Four a.m.," was his impatient reply. "Listen, I have to go back into the city. A client of mine needs me urgently."

I wiped the sleep out of my eyes, registering for the first time his charcoal-black suit and briefcase in hand. "You've got to be kidding me," I murmured, kicking the covers off. Jack took a few steps back. "I didn't even want to come out here but you said this was our little vacation! And now you're zooming back into work-mode. What the fukk, Jack?" I spat at him, pushing past him and padding to the bathroom.

"Don't be so infantile, Sofia. You're thirty-eight, not three, for God's sake," he countered calmly. "Besides, I'll only be a few hours; back by lunch. It's not like you're even going to be up, is it?"

I splashed icy water from tap onto my face, savouring the zing that shot through my nerves. Ignoring Jack only made him angry, and right then, I wanted to annoy the shit out of him. I was hurt beyond relief. Maybe this impromptu getaway was the last chance I had to save our marriage but how could I do that if his work kept getting in the way, vying for his attention and winning?

"Sof? Look, I'm sorry." Jack's voice became softer, apologetic. "Go swimming or something. It'll be sunny today, guaranteed. You're looking pale these days. Get a tan."

I pushed past him and crawled back under the covers. Minutes later, he wrenched them off me.

"I'm talking to you, Sofia. How do you think I can afford this place?" he snarled at me, actually stooping to do it in my ear. "By refusing clients when they need me? By slacking?"

I hated it when he said things like that, made it seem like I was a lazy gold-digger and he was the provider, the one I depended on.

"I could be working, you know," I said softly, hating how petulant my voice sounded. "A nurse's salary is better than nothing."

"Don't start that nonsense again, Sofia. You're starting to piss me off."

"Safe trip, then," I mumbled, keeping my back to him.

The covers were once again draped over me and I heard the soft shuffle of his shoes against the carpet as he walked out.

I didn't realise that I was crying until I tasted the salt.

Go swimming, huh? I thought, scrubbing down between my legs, rough enough to turn the flesh there a flaming red. Is that your idea of a fúcking ball, Jack?

The shower head flung icy needles of water at me and I turned my face up to face them head-on, eyes squeezed shut. If I was lucky, the cold would kill me and I wouldn't have to deal with my husband's absence again.

He'd probably have me cremated. Less hassle.

What was I going to do with myself in this big old house? Holly was out for the day, visiting a niece of hers who just happened to live around here, and now Jack was gone too. Much to Jack's chagrin, year in, year out, I never bonded with any of the smug, pearl-wearing madams of The Comptons, whose idea of fun was sipping sparkling wine and gossiping about whose-husband-fucked-whose-maid.

They were far too stuffy for my liking, and all older than me by far, most in their late forties or early fifties. I had absolutely nothing in common with them. I couldn't care less about horse-riding and tennis and society parties. Hell, I still listened to Daft Punk and watched Dawson's Creek reruns. These old bats probably thought the band was a clothes label.

I reached up and tried to move the shower head about – and it broke apart in my hand, releasing a powerful jet of cold water all over, the pipe falling apart in seconds. Squealing, I jumped back, banging into the glass wall of the shower.

I stood there for a minute, shocked into si-lence until a giggle surged from somewhere in my body. In seconds, I'd destroyed an entire shower system. Stepping out of the shower and towelling myself dry, I headed for the phone at Jack's bedside. He'd be stark-raving mad if he came home to find that I'd completely destroyed the shower, although the thing was probably centuries old and was bound to fall apart some-time.

Jack made it a point to have a handwritten list of emergency numbers by the phone, especially on holidays. I picked up his personalised notepad, scanning the list for something useful.

Emma Biers – Florist

Lloyd Jackson – Gardener/Landscaper

Imogen Waters – Chef

Tracy Kingston – Cleaner

Archibald Parker – Mr. Fix-It

Sarah Pamsy – Masseuse

Trust Jack to have a masseuse on speed-dial. I rolled my eyes at how superficial that was.

Archibald it would be.

"Parker and Associates, how may I help you?" a gruff voice said on the first ring.

"Hi, this is Mrs. Harrington. Um, I live at one of the houses in The Comptons...and the shower's broken."

"Broken? The shower head?"

"Yeah. Among other things. I don't know... It just sort of fell apart." I let out a laugh, catching myself. The man would end up thinking I was a loon. "Sorry."

"For laughing? I find it funny myself. Don't worry, madam. Just give me the address and someone will be there in twenty minutes. Is that all right?"

"Perfect," I replied, even though it wasn't. I took ages to get ready, even for a day of swimming.

After hanging up, I moisturised and threw on a sky-blue Versace dress on, a present from Jack. It was a little too much for a day indoors but I loved this dress. Jack said it brought out the colour of my eyes, which were a shade darker than the flimsy material. I pulled my hair into a messy ponytail and skipped downstairs to the kitchen, stomach growling. The only thing I truly loved about this house was the kitchen, which beat my kitchen at home any day.

This kitchen was old and Victorian, like something out of an old movie. Not much had been changed, aside from the stove and the addition of a few modern necessities, like a refrigerator, microwave and coffee-maker. The floor was gorgeous, granite or some other material, and under my bare feet, it felt like cool heaven.

I had just taken a seat in front of my bagel and coffee when a loud knock resounded. Archibald was nothing if he wasn't prompt. Sighing, I picked up my mug and padded to the front door, wrenching the heavy thing open.

"Archibald?" I asked, even though I knew very well that the man on my doorstep was not Archibald; could not be Archibald.

The man on the phone had sounded old. This man…was young. Yes, very young. From the top of his thick blue-black hair to the soles of his Nike sneakers, he screamed of fun and vitality. A checkered blue-and-white shirt with the sleeves rolled up stretched across a broad chest and shoulders and black jeans hung off lean hips. The greenest eyes I'd ever seen, set off by tanned skin, stared back at me. This was not Archibald.

"Nope, but I am a Parker," he cheerfully replied, a boyish grin on his face. "Uh, can I come in?"

"Oh, right, yes. Please." I stepped aside to let him in, enveloped in some sort of cologne that seemed to linger longer than was necessary.

"Did I interrupt your breakfast?" he asked, waiting patiently for me to close the door.

"No," I lied, taking a sip of my coffee. "Can I make you a cup?"

"Sure. But why don't you show me this crumbling shower first?" he said pleasantly, flashing me another smile.

I nodded, feeling heat stain my cheeks. "Yes. Great."

I went past him, leading the way up to the bedroom. I thought I could feel his eyes on my butt and, for one crazy nanosecond, considered wiggling it a little. Catching the interest of a younger and very attractive male would make up for a lot of things.

All thoughts of making a fool of making a fool of myself flew out the window when I realised what a state the bedroom was in. Making the bed hadn't even occurred to me.

"Sorry about the mess," I muttered, setting my empty mug on the dresser.

He laughed good-naturedly. "Mess? Fuck, you should see my room!" The smile fled from his face. "Christ, sorry. I shouldn't be cursing in front of clients, especially women."

"No, feel free," I told him. "Fúck etiquette."

Surprised green eyes drilled into mine, forcing me to look away.

"Well, here's the bathroom. Obviously," I mumbled quickly, motioning him inside. I opened the steamed-up shower door, revealing the remains of the shower head on the tiles inside.

"Rust. Definitely rust," the man said upon a speedy inspection. He turned to look at me with those eyes of his again. "We'll need a new extension pipe as well. The thing's been silently crumbling away inside the wall."

"Oh?"

"Yup. Mrs. Harrington, I'll do the shopping and give you the bill. Our policy is that you don't pay until the job is done, and not just done – but done properly," he said, his eyes back on the shower.

I felt the strangest pull in my abdomen, a pull I dimly recognised. His words had only been moderately suggestive and yet, my body was responding to them as if they were an actual pick-up line.

"Sofia," I said on impulse.

His head jerked in my direction. "Excuse me?"

"I'm Sofia."

"Are you Spanish?"

It was ridiculous to assume but in this case … "Half," I told him. My father had never even been to Spain, despite his roots and, aside from watching the occasional interactive travel show, neither had I.

Now, this man was reaching out and pushing a lock of hair out of my face. "Which half?" he asked slowly. "This half?" His hand moved down one cheek, down one exposed shoulder, and down my side. My breath caught in my throat. "Or this half?" He moved in, his other hand tracing my other side. For a handyman, his hands were surprisingly soft and delicate. I shivered, puzzled by what he was doing.

"I… Pipe. Are you…going to buy the pipe?" My words came out in a jumble.

He smiled, retracting his hands. It was as if he hadn't just touched me, hadn't just set my hair aflame. "Yeah. Right after that coffee. Remember?"

Oh fúck, I thought, because I didn't know how long I could take this unwelcome torture of staring at him.

"Then we should go to the kitchen," I mumbled, wringing my hands.

"After you," he said, "Sofia."

CHAPTER 3

"Sugar?"

"Just one."

"Milk?"

"Nah."

"Here you go."

"Thank you, Sofia."

Once the coffee was relieved from me, I could finally retreat to a safe distance and observe.

Vaughn – for that was what he'd casually revealed was his name – sat at the kitchen table, a large and dark-haired boy-man, so out of place that it was almost hilarious. He wasn't even my type and, in reality, I was just too old for him to even give me the time of day. And I was married, for goodness' sake!

So I tried to find faults with him, if only to make myself feel better.

His hair was a little too curly, thick, and all over the place; that just-got-outta-bed look. He'd probably never heard of a comb. His nose… Well, his nose was far too pointy, too Phoenician. It stood, proud and sharp, above lips that were too plump to be considered masculine. They disappeared when he took a swig of coffee. No, Vaughn Parker wasn't even on my radar.

But he was delicious to look at.

Dangerously delicious to look at.

"Where's your husband?"

The question was asked as nonchalantly as possible.

I blinked, properly focusing on Vaughn. He was looking at me with interest, like we were about to have a meaningful conversation.

"Working." My reply was curt and, if I thought about it, irritated. Was I pissed off that he was acknowledging my husband, or pissed off that I had a husband in the first place? I wasn't about to think too hard about that.

"Yeah? What does he do?"

"He's a lawyer."

Vaughn nodded. "And he left you all alone." It was a statement, not a question, and I bit my bottom lip.

"He's probably on his way back," I felt the need to say. If I wasn't careful, my nose was going to grow because I knew Jack would be taking his time to get back. "Besides, we don't have to be joined at the hip. We're married, not Siamese twins."

Vaughn let out a laugh. "Fair point, Sofia."

The stirring in my abdomen grew at the way he said my name. It sounded daft, but his tongue seemed to caress all three syllables, almost like a lover would caress –

Stop right there, Sofia Harrington. Stop it! Just stop it!

"How long will fixing up the shower take?" I asked suddenly.

He set the mug down on the table. "Not that long. One day, tops." He paused, giving me a soft look. "Thanks for the coffee. I'll be out of your hair now," he told me, standing up and stretching. The hem of his shirt rode up, revealing a toned bit of brown flesh – and the unmistakable line of a dark happy trail. I swallowed; instantly uncomfortable, instantly appalled by the sudden moisture in my knickers.

"I'll be back in an hour. That all right?" he wanted to know, shoving one hand in his back pocket. He looked down at me questioningly.

"That's fine. I'll be here." I led him back to the front door, eager to see the back of him.

"Good. See you, then."

"Yes. See you."

And I closed the door, leaning against it for support.

What the hell was happening to me? I was acting like a bloody teenager!

You're so turned on you don't know how you'll get off.

The voice in my head was startlingly right. Unfortunately.

Under water, everything was so much simpler.

Nothing mattered, because all there was, was blue, icy-cold water and the blood flowing to my brain. So I guessed Jack was right about swimming being a distraction.

A distraction from a certain green-eyed hunk.

You only met him five seconds ago!

So what? It's not like this is going anywhere.

And what if, by some miracle, that stunt he pulled in the bathroom means he's interested?

I'll let him fuck my brains out, of course!

I swam laps for God-knows-how-long, trying to clear my suddenly-scrambled mind, until my muscles began protesting and I was forced to get out. I grabbed the towel I'd flung onto the chaise longue and dried myself off, wrapping it around my head turban-style once I was done. Instinctively, my head swiveled towards the door on the patio.

Vaughn was standing there, casually leaning against one wall.

I blushed, aware that I was close to being completely naked. My bikini was one size too small and left little to the average predator's imagination. Jack didn't particularly like me wearing it out in public, which is why it was reserved for moments like this. Private moments.

But this was my house. I wasn't going to feel uncomfortable about taking a swim, even if my breasts were spilling out my bikini top.

So I sashayed towards the door, giving Vaughn what I hoped was a seductive smile.

"Did you let yourself in?" I asked the obvious question.

He had the decency to redden. "Sorry. I did knock, though."

"It's OK." I unwrapped the turban, letting my hair fall in a tumble around my shoulders. I pretended to ignore his blatant ogling, when it was making my stomach do somersaults into the deep end of the pool. "You brought the...equipment?"

"Yes, ma'am." He dragged his eyes from my chest. "It's at the foot of the stairs. I've been here for, like, twenty minutes."

I stared at him. "Doing what?"

"Watching you."

I swallowed. "You should have called out to me."

"Doesn't matter anymore, does it?"

"I guess not. You can go up to the bathroom. I don't mind you being there alone."

"OK," he said, and headed back into the house. I hadn't failed to notice that he had changed out of his shirt and into a white wife-beater. It hugged every muscle like an old friend and put the sinewy muscles of his biceps on display.

He's younger than you, my conscience scolded. *Have you no shame?*

"No, I don't," I said aloud, then let out a long sigh. The sad truth was that I was too chicken-shit to do anything. Not only that, my wedding ring was glinting in the sunlight, reminding me that I wasn't Sofia Lopez anymore; I was Mrs.

Jack Harrington. So I could only look. Would only look.

I stalked back into the house, dripping slightly, and went into the kitchen, grabbing a bottle of Evian and taking a long drag. Lunch time was quickly approaching, and Jack was sure to return anytime soon. What would he think of a gorgeous hunk in our bedroom?

I let out a giggle and pulled out one of Holly's homemade lasagnas from the freezer, shoving it into the oven to bake. After that exhausting swim, lunch was my sole priority.

"Mmm… Smells good," a voice said from behind me.

I spun around, nearly giving myself whiplash. "Vaughn. Hey."

"Hey. What are you making?" He strode across the room and peered through the glass of the oven.

"Lasagna. Want some?"

He stood up straight and glanced at me. "Do you want me to have some?"

"We're not in high school, Vaughn. Yes, or no?"

He laughed again. I was beginning to realize that he did that a lot, and that only made him seem even boyish than he probably was. Made it seem like I was perving over a kid.

"Then yeah, I wouldn't mind," he decided, parking himself on a stool at the table. "But listen, I've got to dash out...so I think I'll only be able to really start work on your shower tomorrow. If that's a problem, tell me. I can send someone else in my place." He held eye contact. "If that's what you'd prefer."

I looked away, heading to the cupboard where Holly had put the plates. "No, I'd rather have one person in here."

"Good." His voice sounded much closer...

A cloud of his cologne, which I now recognized as tacky Brut, enveloped me, and then his arms did, too. I stiffened, surprise making the hairs on my arms stand up. His thick arms were around my bare waist, male skin on female, and I finally relaxed, heaving out a sigh.

"Sofia..." His breath was in my right ear and then he was nibbling at my earlobe. I squeezed my eyes shut, breathing heavily at the feel of his lips against my skin. "Sofia, why are you so sad?"

"Sad?" I whispered, as one of his big, soft hands cupped my breast. The thin material made it seem as if he were stroking my hardened nipple. "I'm not." He squeezed, pain shooting through my body, but the sudden dampness in my bikini bottom told a different story.

He slowly removed one bra strap, massaging my arm, and then, with such abruptness, his hand was on my bare breast, teasing my nipple. A low, animal moan escaped my lips; I was beyond the point of no return now.

The other bra strap was pulled down. Vaughn pressed himself against me, the jut of his erection digging into the small of my back. Shock mingled with desire prompted me to lean back into him, eyes still closed, while he worked his magic with his fingers; rubbing, pulling... I was going to burst. I could feel it, and I was sure he could, too.

What are you doing, Sofia?

Oh, shut the fuck up!

"Turn around," he breathed, and I obeyed, forced to look up into those...those eyes. Why did they have such an impact on me? "You are so fucking perfect and I don't think you know that," he said softly, pressed up so close against me I could feel the quick thump of his heart. One of the drawer handles was digging into my spine but I didn't give a shit. No pain, no gain, didn't they say?

"Nobody's perfect," I said quietly, pushing tentative hands up his top. God, those abs – like silk concrete under my fingertips.

"You're not a nobody," he countered, and he lowered his head, his soft lips melding against mine. His tongue dipped across my lower lip, the lightest flicker sending a spike of pleasure through me. My lips parted, letting him in.

He tasted of bubblegum, and I probably still reeked of caffeine, but, judging from the bulge in his pants, he didn't care. Without warning, he picked me up as if I were a bag of air and spun around, laying me flat on the kitchen table.

I caught my breath, trying to sit up, feeling several kinds of awkward. Vaughn gently pushed me back, a sly grin on his face.

"Just close your eyes, Sofia," he commanded, "and relax."

My bikini bottom was gently pulled down to my ankles and my legs pushed apart. Spread-eagled, I had never felt more exposed, more naked. Vaughn positioned himself between my legs, towering above me, his eyes darkening as they took in my bared, pink flesh.

I held my breath, the insecure part of me – the largest part of me – wanted him to like what he saw. Wondered if I'd come up short.

"Hair... I love hair." He let out a soft sigh, stroking my mound. The light touch sent shudders through my body. "Fuck lasagna," he murmured. "I'm having Sofia."

And then, just like that, his face was upon my hot, wet flesh, his tongue flat against my most sensitive parts. The sensation of that tongue flicking against my clit was out of this world. Jack had never eaten me out, and now, here was this...this man doing just that. He held me down for this sweet torture; sucking me, licking, murmuring his enjoyment. I came almost instantly, the sound of my inhibitions being drowned out by my animalistic wail of ecstasy.

Vaughn's big hands were the only things anchoring me to that table and once the aftershocks of my climax had subsided, he kissed my pússy, then slowly kissed his way up my belly, and finally between the parting of my breasts. I stroked the curls of his head, breathing deeply, still trying to wrap my head around the gift he'd just given me.

"Taste yourself," he breathed into my chest before bringing his mouth up to my lips. The salty taste of cum was like a sweet nectar. I hadn't tasted it in...forever.

"I want you," I said on a sigh, pulling away from him. "I want you inside me. Right now. Right here. Bloody hell, screw me!"

He laughed softly, standing straight. "Do you fuck on first dates?"

"I don't care about that!" I hissed, sitting up. "This isn't a date."

He straightened his vest. "See you tomorrow, Sofia Harrington." Wrinkling his nose, he glanced at the oven. "Shit. There goes the lasagna."

I followed his gaze, heaving myself off the table and getting myself back to normal. "Oh, hell. What a waste."

"No," Vaughn whispered, looking me up and down, "this is a waste."

I felt a blush bloom on my cheeks. "Thank you for..." For making me come. For making me feel desirable. I couldn't get the words out.

But he seemed to know what I meant. "You don't have to thank me," he told me, laying a peck on my forehead. "Later, beautiful."

And he was gone, whistling a tune on his way out.

I could still taste myself on my lips, but the smell of his cologne was gone, overpowered by the stench of burnt cheese. It was as if Vaughn Parker never existed.

CHAPTER 4

"Mrs. Harrington?"

I poked my head out from under the covers.

"What?" I mumbled, wincing in the sunlight. The curtains had been pulled apart and the sunlight that poured in was near blinding.

"Mr. Harrington told me to tell you that he does not want to be disturbed this morning. He is in his study," Holly recited, standing patiently at my bedside. "May I bring you breakfast in bed?"

"I won't disturb him," I muttered irritably, sitting up and yawning. "And yes, that would be great."

Holly nodded and turned on her heel, humming to herself. She really was a doll and I had no idea what I would've done without her.

Smiling, I went to the bathroom, splashing water on my face and brushing my teeth. The broken shower caught my eye, and I couldn't help the burst of energy that fizzed through my entire body. This shower was a reminder.

A reminder of the day before.

"Malfunction in the bathroom," I'd simply told Jack when he finally reappeared late in the afternoon, half-hearted apologies on his lips. "I'm taking care of it."

"Well, this is an old house," he'd responded. "You called Archibald?"

"Mm-hmm."

"All right."

And that was that. Jack didn't particularly mind taking a bath in the large claw-foot tub. It wasn't like it was torture.

In fact, I needed a bath myself. What happened yesterday had confused me. I'd expected to be guilt-ridden; absolutely disgusted and disappointed by the way I'd behaved. Getting head was considered cheating, no matter how hard I tried to convince myself otherwise. I spent the whole evening wondering if Jack was going to notice, whether he was going to see that this woman – well – this woman had had her pússy eaten, and it was not by him.

But he didn't.

He barely came near me, save for a chaste peck on the forehead before bed and promises to spend time with me the next day. And, for the first time in a long time, I was completely fine with that. Hell, I even preferred it that way.

Completely nude after a quick bath, I left the bathroom to find a tray of English breakfast set on the nightstand with my birth control. My stomach rumbled in anticipation. Holly was gorgeous.

It was while stuffing my face with bacon-on-toast that Jack came in, dressed in a blue shirt and khaki slacks, an anxious expression on his face. "What are you doing?" he asked, looking me up and down.

"Building a tree-house? What does it look like?"

"Don't get cute. Didn't you say Parker's coming to fix the bathroom early this morning? What if he walks in and finds you stark-naked?"

"Then I'll make his day." I rolled my eyes up at him. "What's up with you?"

"I've got a bit of work to do." He rummaged through one suitcase until he located a handful of khaki envelopes. "Please don't disturb me," he said, looking up.

"I wouldn't fucking dream of it," I fumed. Why was he treating me like a child? Scratch that, why did I let him?

Because he's Jack and he was your first and you desperately want this to work despite every-thing.

My husband nodded and turned on his heel, slamming the door behind him. I flopped back onto the bed, trying to rein in my anger. If I didn't, I'd go after him and tell him exactly what he could do with his bloody work.

But Jack wasn't the one who'd climaxed all over the kitchen table with another man's head between his legs.

"Mrs. Harrington?" Holly stood in the doorway watching me make the bed. "The plumber's here. Shall I send him up?"

I always seemed to forget this vital action of cleaning a room and I wanted to make sure I got it done before Vaughn came up.

"Yes. Please," I replied, a bit too cheerfully for my liking. "Is, um, Jack still in the study?"

"I believe so."

"OK. Well… Send the…plumber up, I guess."

I gave myself a critical look-over in the mirror. Maybe my dress was a little too short. Maybe I looked a little too put together. Maybe Jack would come in and see right through me.

Then again, Vaughn's hands running up my exposed thighs would feel so good…

"Hey."

Speak of the devil.

Today, he was in a white T-shirt and checkered board shorts that fell just above his knees. His hair was unrulier than it had been yesterday, dark curls straying over his forehead. I just about dissolved in pure desire.

"Morning," I said, forcing some normalcy into my voice. I swallowed when he closed the bedroom door behind him.

"Sleep well?" He strode into the bathroom and began rummaging through his toolbox, leaving the door open.

"I did." And I had. Sated by my orgasm and guilt-free, I'd slumbered peacefully. "You?"

"Always."

I pretended to busy myself with folding some random clothes, steadfastly ignoring his presence in the bathroom.

"Your husband home?"

I glanced in his direction. "Yes. In the next room. Working."

"I'd like to meet this workaholic." He chuckled. "Beginning to think he doesn't exist."

"I'll...I'll be back," I stuttered. I just could not do this. Be around him. And pretend that I wasn't horny. That I didn't want to fúck him.

So I hurried out the room and flew downstairs. I just had to busy myself with something. It didn't matter what as long as it kept my mind off actually having full-on sex with a man I'd only known for twenty-four hours.

I found Holly in the kitchen, doing the washing up.

"Do we have any baking ingredients?" I asked her.

She gave me a strange look. "It depends on what you want to bake, Mrs. Harrington."

I bit my lip. "A cake."

"Yes, but what kind of cake?"

I thought about it. "Chocolate? Yes. Chocolate. A moist chocolate cake."

She gave me a candid look. "I can make that for you. You don't –"

"No," I said firmly, then sighed. "Holly, I'm useless in the kitchen. I just have to learn. Is there a cookbook around here?"

She dried her hands with a dishcloth and rifled through some drawers, producing an ancient cookbook and handing it to me. "This is an Alfreda Jefferson classic. It has some of the oldest recipes known to woman."

I took it from her. "As long as there aren't any bat wings involved, it'll do."

She smiled warmly. "Are you baking for Mr. Harrington?"

I nodded. "Yes. I just feel like doing something...womanly."

After sitting at the kitchen table and paging through the book for a suitable recipe, I came to the conclusion that the kitchen was no place for someone like me. Just what the hell were all the measurements for? Did it matter how much sugar you used? Couldn't you use your discretion? I mean, no one wanted to overdo sweetness, unless they wanted to put themselves in an early grave, right?

Sighing, I carried the book up with me upstairs, pausing at the door of Jack's study.

If I knock, he's definitely going to bite my head off, and then some.

I grudgingly returned to our bedroom, sitting at the vanity table. Vaughn had shoved earphones into his ears and was now hammering away at the shower wall. I got to work rearranging my toiletries on the table. I couldn't live out of a suitcase like Jack could; it just wasn't right. I always unpacked, even if we stayed at a hotel.

"What are you doing?"

I glanced at the bathroom. Vaughn was giving me a quizzical look.

"Cleaning," I replied.

"Is this how you spend your mornings on holiday?"

I blushed. "Of course not. I'm just... I'm –"

"Sofia."

There he went, saying my name that way. I turned in my seat, looking at the open bedroom door. Vaughn took that opportunity to come at me from my side.

"You look tense," he said simply.

Oh God.

"Vaughn, don't."

His hands were on my shoulders, and he slow-ly began kneading the muscles there. I uttered a low moan, squeezing my eyes shut, succumbing to the instant pleasure. All thoughts of my husband in the next room and maid downstairs flew out the window, along with the small twinge of guilt.

But then, when Vaughn's hands began to wan-der towards my aching breasts, a wave of thick shame washed over me. I jumped up, breathing heavily. I was married. My husband was a wall away!

"Please stop," I whispered, picking up the cookbook, intent on heading to the kitchen and being a good little wife. Maybe I'd make a sim-ple vanilla cake.

Vaughn turned me around, eyes trained on me. "Do you really want me to stop, Sofia?"

No, I thought to myself. No, I want to throw you onto the bed and ride you until Jack comes in, wondering what the hell is going on.

No. "Yes. I do. Please, Vaughn. This isn't right."

He arched a brow. "Sofia. You want me."

"Yes, but wanting and having you are two different things," I murmured, trying to fight against the things he was making me feel.

I was married, I was much older than him, I was sure, and someone like Vaughn – someone so sure of himself – was going to be bored with little Sofia Lopez who'd only ever fúcked one man; a man who didn't seem to want to fúck her anymore.

Vaughn kicked the stool aside, and it fell to the floor with a loud thud. Pressing himself up against me, I held the cookbook to my chest like a lifesaver. His breath was on my neck.

"W-what are you doing?" I breathed, aware that my eyes were widening to saucer-like pro-portions. His lips were on my skin, his breath warm and titillating.

"I will savour every part of your body; every nook and every cranny Sofia," he murmured into my skin. "I will make you feel like my last meal, make you want to be eaten. And I will do it with your husband in the next room." His tongue flickered out, electrocuting me almost instantaneously.

"Vaughn," I sighed, lost, completely lost to him.

"Where can we go, Sofia?" he breathed. "I have to have you. Today. You think I slept a fucking wink last night? Think again. Cold shower after cold shower, and I couldn't get rid of this." He brought my hand to the bulge in his pants. "Tell me you want me, Sofia. Just say it. Admit it."

I couldn't breathe, couldn't perform the simple act I needed to do to live. Could desire make your lungs malfunction?

"The attic," I heard myself saying, squeezing his cóck through his shorts. "No one will go up there."

"Then let's go."

I took his hand and led him out the room.

CHAPTER 5

The floorboards protested under our feet. Too loud for comfort.

What if Jack investigates? The scary thought made goosebumps prickle my skin.

But he wouldn't. Once Jack went into his study, he might as well have been in a different dimension. Simple as that.

I hadn't had any time to explore this attic before now, but it was extremely spacious. A bunch of old furniture had been shoved up here and forgotten about, so dust was abundant.

As were cobwebs. And, perhaps, rats.

"Maybe...maybe we should –"

Vaughn pressed his lips against mine, shutting me up and pushing me against one wall. I felt my will crumble as I laced my arms around his waist, my hands disappearing up his shirt.

His hands were suddenly slipping up the hem of my dress, dancing up my thighs. I ached with the need to feel him at my centre, and squeezed my eyes shut when he began to play with the elastic of my panties. They were black lace, the sexiest pair I owned, and I hadn't realised that I'd worn them for him until he was actually fingering them.

"How many times do you think I can make you come?" he whispered into my ear, one hand slipping into my underwear and lightly brushing against my warmth.

"I...don't...know..." I breathed, desire pooling in my abdomen.

"Once?" One finger slipped inside me. I shuddered with aroused surprise, grasping at him for support. "Twice?" Two fingers. "Three times?" Three fingers now, stretching me almost uncomfortably. "Shit. You are incredibly tight for a non-virgin," Vaughn declared, releasing a low groan.

Because I can count on one hand how many times my husband and I have had sex.

Vaughn removed one finger and slowly rubbed the pad of his thumb over my swollen clit, increasing the pressure bit by bit. I silently told myself not to come but couldn't fight the mini orgasm that swept through me. It left me panting, amazed that I could come so quickly, so unexpectedly. Opening my eyes, I found Vaughn staring at me.

"I wish you could see yourself," he said softly.

"What?"

"You look shocked. Like you can't believe you're actually coming." He removed his hand and brought his wet fingers to his mouth. "Shit, Sofia..." Taking my hand, he brought it to the fly of his pants, where the bulge of his cock was straining to be free.

I thought of something.

"You've tasted me," I said huskily, kneeling before him, "but I haven't tasted you."

He looked down at me, a smirk on his face. "Well, since you're in the neighbourhood..."

I unzipped his fly, the anticipation making me shiver. His boxers were pinstriped cotton and as I unwrapped his length and released it from its confines, he released a painful groan.

He was huge, that much was evident.

Much, much bigger than Jack.

I had a moment of uncertainty because I'd never done this before. What if I'm rubbish at it? What if I accidentally bite down and he sues me? Being "experimental" just wasn't in the vocabulary of my sex life with my husband. Jack was strictly a "three-minute-missionary" man – so there was never any room for oral.

Vaughn mistook my worry for reluctance. "You don't have to do this, Sofia," he said gently, running his hands through my hair. "I enjoy making you come."

"I want to," I told him, keeping my eyes on his erection. It looked daunting; impressively thick and red and leaking a clear fluid. But I wanted it.

Sol took a deep breath and slowly eased him inside my mouth, until the head was kissing the back of my throat before I drew him out. He was salty on my tongue; spicy, even. Since I'd never had a man's c0ck in my mouth, I used my imagination, exploring every raised vein, every inch of silky steel.

"Oh, sweetheart," he groaned, laying one hand on the back of my head to hold me there as he slowly rocked back and forth.

Pleasure lanced through him when I realised that this was good for him. Gently, I scraped his shaft with my teeth, making Vaughn grip a clump of my hair in his hand and pull. I expected pain to shoot through my head from this savage act but there was nothing, only the feel of my soaked panties. Pleasuring someone else was giving me pleasure.

"You're gonna make me come." His hips pistoned forward, faster than before. Breathing raggedly, he told me how good I was at sucking him off, how much he wanted to fill my dirty little mouth with his cum.

His filthy words sent shivers of delight down my spine and I squeezed my eyes shut, teasing him, tasting him, until finally, he exploded in my mouth, his large body racking.

His fluid filled my mouth, and for a minute, I thought I would choke but instinct told me to clamp down and allow Vaughn to slide himself out my mouth when he was done.

I swallowed.

"Fúck," Vaughn breathed, pulling me to my feet. His hands instantly pulled my dress up over my head. "You're beautiful – do you know that?" he said softly, pushing me up against the wall. We were in between two old couches, dusty and tattered from age and neglect, but I felt as though we were on top of the Eiffel Tower.

That was exactly how he was making me feel.

Vaughn leaned in and nuzzled into my neck, the smell of his shampoo – something with apricot – wafted into my nostrils. It was such an aphrodisiac my pússy was dripping in earnest.

I let my hands play with his hardening cóck, enjoying the way he trembled from my every touch. I stroked his shaft, cupping his balls in my hand. Squeezing, I heard his gasp of shock and, satisfied that I affected him as much as he affected me, I released him.

"Sofia, Sofia... You're a different breed," he breathed, unhooking my bra from behind. He pulled it off, staring at my breasts for a long, uncomfortable moment. Then, he lowered his head to pull one nipple into his mouth.

I had to bite my lip to stop the wail I knew was just aching to escape. My breasts felt heavy and swollen, and the warmth of his mouth on one just about turned me to pulp. He moved to my neglected breast, his fingers teasing the other, ensuring that neither was left untouched. I had my hands in his hair, pulling, and then, in a flash, he tugged my knickers down my thighs.

Stepping out of them, I was completely and utterly naked.

If Jack came up, there would be no doubt about what was going on.

Vaughn came up for air, his eyes dark and shameless.

He took a step back and his eyes raked my body.

All my insecurities flashed through my mind – my breasts, my butt, my tummy...

"You shouldn't wear clothes," Vaughn told me, taking a step forward.

"You look silly," I said gently, reaching for his shorts and tugging, "with this hanging out."

He chuckled, digging in his back pockets and coming out with a foil packet. "Then come here."

This is going to happen. No matter what, this is going to happen.

Vaughn's lips met mine in a soft kiss and my lips parted slightly, letting his tongue slide in to tangle with mine. My breath rushed out when he shoved me into the wall, cupping my butt and lifting me.

"You ready, sweet Sofia?" This was whispered against my lips.

My eyes shut. "God, yes." And I was. So wet, so ready, so willing.

I felt him smile against my lips. Then I couldn't have cared less about his mouth because he was slowly easing into me, opening me up like I'd never felt before.

"Baby, you're so tight."

I whimpered, looping my arms around his neck, so dizzy from sensation I would have detached from him if I didn't hold on.

"Such a tight little pússy." Vaughn pushed in to the hilt, so abruptly my eyes snapped open and I had to stifle my moan against his mouth.

Behind me, the wall was cold, but in front of me and inside me, this man was scorching and setting every inch of me on fire.

"Please, Vaughn," I begged, digging my nails into his back when his groin met my clít. "Please...fúck me."

"I am, Sofia. Fúck, I am."

The air was filled with my sobs of pleasure, with his low growls of satisfaction. I could smell his sweat, smell the scent of my juices coating his sheathed cOck. It was heady and I found myself murmuring gibberish a few times, drowning in the pool of pleasure he was dunking me in.

Vaughn was big; he filled me up completely, so it wasn't a huge shocker when, minutes later, I experienced the best climax of my poor sexually starved existence. Vaughn followed seconds later on a muffled shout, his face pressed into my heaving chest.

I had to stifle my screams and, when it was over, I was reduced to a gasping mess, sweat pouring down my back in rivulets. Still inside me, this boy-man carried me over to one dusty couch, and eased himself into a sitting position. Now, sitting on top of him, I was the boss.

And it felt so good.

"Do you feel guilty?" Vaughn wanted to know, stroking my bare arms.

His question threw me. But the truth was harder to accept. "No."

Inside me, his cóck was stirring to life again and in this position, I felt...fuller. It felt incredible to have him like this, to know that I was making him like this.

Vaughn's eyes were knowing, like he knew exactly what I was thinking. "Will you fúck me now, Sofia?"

Desire had a noose around my throat. Placing one hand on each armrest, I raised myself off him until he was partially inside me then, without warning, came back down on him, overflowing with his length. A groan escaped his lips while I did it again and again, until I worked out a rhythm that was beginning to liquefy my insides. Riding him set off a chain reaction of mini climaxes, one after the other, and I wanted more, wanted to feel alive again and again.

Time seemed to pass, but it had no meaning in that attic until, finally, I was too spent to even blink. Breathing rapidly, I practically collapsed on top of him. It felt right when his arms came around me and he kissed my earlobe.

"I don't think I'll finish that shower today," he whispered into my ear, his hands running along my spine.

"I don't think so, either," I breathed, kissing his shoulder.

"Then we have a problem."

"We do."

"I'll have to come over again tomorrow."

"Definitely," I said firmly, sitting up properly. He placed his hands on my waist.

"I'm hard again," he said quietly, looking into my eyes.

"Yes, I can feel that," I replied, my voice suddenly hoarse and leaned in to kiss his lips. "And I don't think that's normal."

For three more days, our shower remained unfixed – and Jack asked no questions. His free time was stolen by some old chums of his, stuffy men in their mid-forties who wore slacks and cardigans in this heat. I was glad that he'd abandoned his work in the study and had started going out and being more sociable, but this meant that I was expected to go out and be more sociable, too.

Still, whenever Vaughn was around, we'd slip upstairs into the attic and have a quickie on a couch. In fact, the day after our first tryst, I'd sneaked upstairs with some cleaning agents, dusting the place and airing it as best as I could. If it was to become a place of pleasure, it had to at least smell good.

I learned very quickly that Vaughn could be gentle, aggressive, playful, caring and attentive during lovemaking. I loved his aggressive side, because it meant that there was a tiny element of danger. If he bit me too hard, the telltale marks would show. If he rammed into me too hard, I probably wouldn't be able to walk for days.

The danger of Jack guessing that I'd been with the handyman thrilled me, for reasons I couldn't explain. Perhaps it had something to do with how he thought he controlled every aspect of my life. But this? He didn't control what I was doing with Vaughn. He had no idea.

"No, Sofia. Wear the purple dress. It's better than that ghastly red affair," Jack was saying as we got ready for yet another idiotic cocktail at the pier. One of his friends, an overweight German called Gunter, was having a meaningless birthday party to be celebrated onboard the Fraulein Maria.

All The Comptons bigwigs were going to be there, which was why Jack wanted me to make a special effort. But I despised the purple dress he wanted me to wear.

It was just too mature, which was why Jack adored it. The idea of resembling one of my ancestors didn't appeal to me in the slightest.

"I prefer this one, Jack," I said calmly, smoothing down the front of my dress. It was red and knee-length, with big black roses splattered all over. It was one of the few things I'd bought for myself; one of the few things that was actually me.

"Fine," he grunted reluctantly. "Wear the gaudy thing. Let's go."

I'm sick and tired of your mood swings, I thought, glaring after him. I wished I had the courage to say it aloud.

Gunter van der Venter knew how to throw a party.

For a fiftieth birthday bash, it was beginning to look like a sweet sixteen soiree. As one of the few bachelors in the Comptons, he'd brought in a few girlfriends from the city – tall, model-like girls who intimidated the stuffy older Comptons bunch.

Still, the alcohol was a welcome addition, and I made sure to glue myself to the bar, once Jack found someone to talk business with, of course. His work bored me to tears and I was glad that he'd discovered someone else to boast to about the embezzlement case he was currently working on.

"What can I get you, ma'am?" the bartender asked, a wide grin on his face. "You look like you could use something strong."

I laughed. "Tequila, please," I told him, settling into a bar stool and making myself comfy. "And keep it coming."

He raised a brow but went to work.

Four straight shots later, and I was feeling slightly tipsy. I wasn't the best drinker out there and this was why my husband "advised" me to stick to non-alcoholic drinks when we went out. Today, though... Today, I didn't give a damn what Jack thought. I needed a drink because I deserved one, damn it. Fucking a guy whose stamina rivalled that of a prized stallion took a lot of energy.

Still, I didn't want to get so shit-faced I ended up confessing my adultery. Just when I was about to switch to soda, a familiar deep voice rumbled out a "Whisky, please," from beside me.

My head jerked to my right.

He was in a black suit, no tie. His white shirt was unbuttoned, the tan of his skin appearing golden in the sun. And he looked utterly and completely gorgeous.

"What are you doing here?" I asked, my tongue rolling the 'R's emphatically.

Vaughn stared down at me, a smile breaking across his face. "Sofia Harrington, are you drunk?"

"Perhaps."

"You still look beautiful," he said, downing his drink in one gulp. "Oh, how I needed that." He set the empty glass back onto the counter.

"Refill?" the bartender asked.

Vaughn shook his head in response, his eyes trained on me.

"Are you enjoying yourself?" The question was asked so that only I could hear him.

I shook my head. I hated being surrounded by all these people I didn't have a thing in common with. I hated the fact that I had been allowed to wear this dress. But most of all, I hated that my body actually sang when Vaughn called me beautiful.

"Come with me. I want to show you something." He stretched his hand out.

Without thinking, I took it.

His mouth was against mine.

Throwing me onto the bed, he hiked my dress up and dragged my thong down my legs.

"Spread your legs for me and show me how wet you are, Sofia," he demanded, standing over the bed.

I wondered how obscene I looked, with my dress pulled up my waist and my legs apart, baring my sopping wet pússy. The alcohol certainly lowered my inhibitions, made it so that I didn't feel awkward and unattractive.

I was wanton and filthy and when Vaughn groaned at the sight of my cúnt, even stroking himself through his pants, I played with my pulsing clít.

"Sofia," Vaughn growled, whipping his wallet out and snagging a square packet from inside. "Such a good little girl." His pants were un-zipped.

Little girl? I'm older than you, Vaughn. And I don't ever want to find out how old you are.

The unwelcome thought made what I was do-ing feel silly and I stopped playing with myself, receiving a pointed stare from Vaughn.

"What, baby?"

"I..."

"Stop thinking," he commanded, already sheathing himself. "We both want me inside your sweet cúnt, yes?"

"Yes." I sighed when his weight was on the bed, between my legs, his cOck erect and thick.

"Good, because I can't wait."

Seconds later, he was buried inside me, hoisting my legs onto his shoulders. This was our first time on an actual bed and this unusual position – to me, at least – made the experience otherworldly. For the first time, we could make as much noise as we wanted; the noises from the top deck swallowed up our moans.

Vaughn was rabid with his thrusts, demanding me to fúck him, to swallow his cOck with my tight cúnt. The bed groaned and moaned beneath us, protesting its assault, and for a second, I was afraid we'd break it.

I came harder than ever before, sobbing my pleasure. Maybe it was the excitement of doing the nasty in Gunter van der Venter's bedroom on Gunter van der Venter's boat at Gunter van der Venter's birthday party.

With my husband right upstairs.

Or maybe it was just being with Vaughn like this, in a bed.

"Oh God," I said hoarsely, when I couldn't take anymore. Vaughn rolled off me, his breathing ragged.

"Feeling better?" he asked, his hand on my bare thigh.

"What do you think?" I giggled, nuzzling into his neck and pecking him there.

"We should get out of here." He sat up, pulling his pants back on.

I pulled my thong up and got off the bed, straightening my dress. My hair and make-up were probably a mess, and my handbag was still at the bar. Hopefully.

I tried to get past Vaughn to leave the room when he grabbed my arm and spun me around, pulling me into a passionate kiss. I was breathless when he finally pulled away.

"What...was...that for?"

His eyes sparkled. "I don't know. I just felt like it."

Something swirled inside me.

Not lust.

Not affection.

Love?

Too fúcking soon and a few years too late, Sofia.

I shook the idea out of my head and turned on my heel and left, my head ringing. Just because a man was showing me affection, didn't mean my stupid little heart could go around getting ideas.

CHAPTER 6

A few days later, Jack was standing in front of the mirror, buttoning up a riding shirt. "Harriet Periwinkle has invited you over for brunch," he said offhandedly, glancing at my reflection in the bed behind him

"Harriet who?" I asked lazily, stifling a yawn. A look at my phone revealed that it had just gone past seven.

"You know her. Her husband owns the stables over by the lake. That's where I'm heading to right now." Jack paused, running a comb through his neatly-cut mousy-brown hair. "He has a delightful thoroughbred that I –"

"Spare me," I muttered, receiving a sharp look. I sighed. "I have to supervise the plumber, remember?" Supervise his díck, that is.

"Speaking of which," Jack said, glancing at the open door of the bathroom, "how long is this supposed to take? I'm tired of the bathtub."

I reddened and hid my face from him. "Oh, I don't know. Old houses like this...There must be other rot and whatnot."

"You might be right. At any rate, I trust Archibald. He hires only the best."

"Exactly. So...I can't possibly go out with Harriet today. I'll phone and let her know. Once I'm fully awake of course."

"Fair enough. I'll be back quite late, though."

"That's okay."

"Sure?" He gave me a curious look, obviously shocked that I wasn't throwing a tantrum.

"Positive," I said. "Absolutely positive."

"Ever thought about piercing these things?" Vaughn tweaked one of my nipples with his fingers. I leaned back into him, turning off the tap with my feet.

"Ever thought about piercing this?" I shot one hand underwater beneath me and grabbed his cóck.

He jumped. "You're mental," he said, chuckling softly, wrapping his arms around my waist.

"Well, so are you."

I felt his mouth on the side of my neck. Squeezing my eyes shut, I relaxed. We ended up going for another round – our third – and making a mess of the bathroom in the process. I was glad that Holly had gone to see her niece – who wasn't feeling well – again. Otherwise she'd have definitely heard the noises and put two and two together. I loved and trusted Holly, but I couldn't ask her to keep a secret like this. It just wasn't fair.

Sex in the bathtub was a whole other experience. Vaughn was another experience. He could make me climax more times in one session than in my whole marriage to my husband. I loved it – and hated it, because what was I going to do when this holiday was over?

"Jack asked me why the shower was taking so long to get fixed," I gasped, riding him for what felt like the billionth time that morning. Vaughn's hands tightened on my hips as he thrust upwards, his cOck finding a place that hadn't ever been reached before.

"What did you tell him?" he grunted.

My grip on the sides of the tub tightened as I felt the beginnings of a massive orga$m coming along. Vaughn's hand came around and dipped underwater, between my thighs, finding my clít and rubbing it. And just like that, he flung me over the precipice and I came, crying his name.

"That it's a fucking old house," I panted in response to his question after I'd come down to earth with a bang.

"It's ancient," he groaned, before his own plea-sure consumed him and he was squeezing the life out of me. "Good girl."

The urge to remind him that I was two decades away from being a girl was strong. Still, I loved it when he called me that. It was such a turn-on to be called a good girl. Or, even better, a bad one. Most of the time, I was bad.

"My skin's getting pruned," I breathed, getting off him and slowly pulling myself to my feet. Vaughn stared up at me, desire in his dazzling jade eyes once more. "And no, we're not screwing again. You need to work on this shower."

"OK, OK." He got up in one fluid motion, removing the condom. Looking down at me, he laid a kiss on my forehead. "I find you extremely sexy, Mrs. Harrington."

I reddened. I did not need the reminder of my husband. "Sofia. It's Sofia. Just Sofia."

"I find it pretty sexy to be fúcking a married woman," he breathed in my ear. He chuckled, stepping out the bathtub to dispose of the condom. Then he grabbed my towel, wrapped it around his waist and headed back into the bedroom, where we'd first had sex that morning.

I made a mental note to take care of the incriminating latex in the bin.

Just what is wrong with you, Sofia? I thought to myself, shaking my head and getting out the tub as well. Naked and dripping, I followed him back into the bedroom.

He'd already pulled on his boxers, his back to me. Once again, I admired his long, youthful body. What was a man like him doing with a woman like me? Vaughn struck me as one of those sex-crazed playboys with boyish charm and c0cks of steel who only targeted gazelle-like blondes.

So where did I, a married, unfit older woman, come into the picture?

"Sofia, put some clothes on. Or I'll have to eat you," Vaughn was saying, a smirk on his face. It was only then that I realised that he was fully-clothed while I was standing nude, drooling over him like a pubescent teenager.

I picked my towel up from the carpet and quickly dried myself up, aware of Vaughn sitting on the bed and watching me. I wanted to tell him to go away.

"You need help with that?" he asked as I rubbed in my sunscreen.

"Nope."

"I think you do," he said determinedly, and came to stand behind me. "Give me that."

"Vaughn, I really don't –"

The bottle was snatched from me and I shut my mouth, watching our reflections in the mirror. Mine shivered in anticipation; his got to work rubbing the cream onto my shoulders. Just the gentlest, lightest touch was an electric shock to my entire body.

Vaughn was gentle, rubbing the sunscreen into every bit of my body that was likely to be exposed to the sun's scorching rays. His hands cupped my breasts, carefully massaging them, playfully teasing my nipples. Uninhibited, I released a low moan, leaning back into him.

I felt that he was hard once again.

Without talking, I turned around and unbuttoned the fly of his shorts as he mashed his mouth against mine, already following my train of thought. Pushing me back into the vanity table, he swept my cosmetics onto the floor and set me on top of it. I should've been annoyed about my spilled perfume, but not right then. I was too wet to care about such trivial things. Again. With that thought, Vaughn entered me with such force that I let out a scream, biting down on his lip, hard enough to draw blood.

Wrapping my legs around his waist and leaning back against the mirror, I experienced a quick and almost painful climax. Vaughn followed, his shout stifled with his mouth on my skin. Gasping for air, he lifted me up, still semi-erect inside me, and gently set me on the bed, meshing his body against mine. I ran my hands through his hair, still panting.

Staring into each other's eyes like this was not part of the deal, but that's exactly what we were doing. Once again, I was struck by how beautiful his eyes were; how vivacious.

And then the door opened.

With great effort, Vaughn pulled out of me, still hard, and I jumped up, grabbing my towel and wrapping it around me.

A tall, golden-haired woman stood in the doorway, a straw basket in hand. She blinked in shock at the two of us.

"I...I heard... The scream," Harriet Periwinkle said, her gaze staying on Vaughn. "Jack said you wouldn't be able to make it for brunch, so I brought it to you." She held up the basket, her lined face flushing. "Er...I'll be downstairs?"

Oh God. This is not happening.

"Yeah. Could you...could you wait in the kitchen?" I asked, matching her rouge skin tone.

"Of..of course." She closed the door behind her.

This is horrible, I thought furiously, getting up. I shot a glare at Vaughn, who had a big grin on his face.

"What's so funny?" I spat, thoughts of Harriet blabbing to Jack racing through my mind. She'd tell him, wouldn't she? And then Jack would... He'd leave me. Or he'd do the thing he'd done once. The thing I swore had never happened...

Vaughn let out a short bark of laughter. "Did you see her eyes on my dick?"

CHAPTER 7

I had only actually met Harriet Periwinkle once before.

As Jack had been quick to point out, her husband (whatever his name was) owned the stables beside the Comptons Lake, ergo the Periwinkles were a very wealthy couple – and extremely stuck-up and old-fashioned, at least from what little I'd seen.

So it was no wonder I was shaking in my glad-iator sandals as I made my way into my kitchen. Harriet Periwinkle was the last person I'd ever wanted to discover me spread-eagled before my plumber. Not that I actually ever wanted anyone to find out about this little affair – but that was beside the point.

Peeking through the entranceway, I spotted Harriet Periwinkle sitting at the table, sipping a large glass of what I could see was pulp orange juice. She'd quickly made herself right at home without my say-so. Dressed in a silk cream blouse and tan slacks, she looked exactly like the pompous Stepford wife I knew she was. Everything about her screamed opulence and sophistication, and it greatly intimidated me. I didn't have any idea of what she would say.

I cleared my throat and went in, pasting a wide smile on my face. "Is the juice OK?" The cheer in my voice was forced but Harriet looked up at me, smiling back.

"I hope you don't mind, dear," she said serenely, raising the glass.

"Not at all," I countered, going into the fridge myself and getting out the jug for myself. I avoided eye contact as I went to get a glass. Perhaps if I did that long enough, she'd dissipate into thin air and I could pretend she had never been here, never even existed.

"Is that young Vaughn Parker upstairs?" she asked after a long moment of silence had passed.

I glanced at her."Er, yes… He's doing the shower."

"Oh? Broken, is it?"

"Very."

She nodded sagely. "Understandable. This house is as old as the hills, as are most of the others."

"Mrs. Periwinkle –" I began.

"I won't tell, you know," she said gently, blue eyes sincere.

"You…you won't?" I asked loudly. The hammering had started up again upstairs and neither of us could act as though Vaughn wasn't in my bedroom after fúcking me.

"Of course not." Harriet waved a hand. "We all need…a release. Besides, dear Jack doesn't seem much fun, does he?"

"He... I... I don't make it a habit, Mrs. Peri-winkle," I finished lamely, knowing that I was blushing like a boil.

"Please, call me Harriet. We're just girls here. You have my word, dear – my lips are sealed."

Lucky. I'm so fucking lucky, I thought to myself, breathing an audible sigh of relief.

I gulped down the bitter juice in one swig, wiping my mouth when I was done. Smoothing down the hem of my dress, I started to think of ways to get her to leave, now that I knew that my secret was safe with her. Between my legs, there was the slightest trickle of liquid, and I experienced a miniature heart attack when I re-membered that Vaughn hadn't used protection before Harriet caught us.

My chest constricted. I was clean – you couldn't get disease from your hand – but was Vaughn? How was I supposed to know he wasn't shagging every married, single, widowed or di-vorced woman in town? Obviously, his morals were...loose and I had no right to assume he used protection with every woman he was with.

The only plus side of this was that I was still taking birth control but the Pill wasn't any protection from STDs...

Shít, shít, shít...

It was then that I noticed Harriet rising to her feet.

Maybe she's leaving. Maybe she can take a hint, the hopeful voice in my head said. Because I had to go right back upstairs and interrogate my bloody plumber about where his díck had been lately.

"I would guess you to be in your...mid-thirties, Sofia," Harriet said out of the blue as she approached me. "A good ten years younger than the rest of us old hags. And much, much prettier."

Standing before me, I realised that she hadn't Botoxed her face like her counterparts – crows' feet were stamped near her eyes when she smiled, a few wrinkles pulled at her lips – and she was much prettier for it.

And then those same lips were on mine.

What the hell is happening?

I was frozen to the spot, eyes wide open in shock, unable to understand what was going on. And when I did, revulsion coiled in my belly. This was an absolute nightmare. Harriet's lips were foreign and unusual and my body would not – could not – respond. Realising this, she pulled away, her face turning a deep shade of red.

"Oh God. Forgive me, Sofia?"

"Are you…are you attracted to me?" I spluttered in disbelief.

She shook her head quickly, her blonde hair staying in place in its French braid. "I don't know what's come over me. I must go. Enjoy the basket." She grabbed her handbag off the table and practically sprinted d out the kitchen, head bent.

The way my day was looking, I definitely needed something stronger to drink.

Dinner with Jack just sent me on a guilt trip and a half. The fact that he was being so damn nice certainly didn't help matters. Holly was back from her niece's place and had made a delicious pasta for dinner. Red wine and pasta were the perfect combination, in my opinion, but

I was afraid to get too drunk in case I blurted something crazy like, "I'm sleeping with the plumber!" or "Your buddy's wife kissed me!"

I was such a lightweight it was humiliating.

"Is everything OK?" Jack asked, sipping his wine.

"Of course," I said quickly. "Why? Do I look strange?"

"You seem a little tense."

Since when do you notice? I thought bitterly, pushing a strand of hair out of my face.

"I'm fine."

"You're not bored, are you?"

"No." And I really wasn't. When Vaughn wasn't inside me, he was actually quite interesting. Surprisingly smart and always witty. He made me laugh and truthfully, his being younger was easy to forget sometimes.

"Harriet Periwinkle told me she stopped by," Jack said lightly. "Wasn't that nice of her?"

"Very." Don't blush, Sofia. Forget about everything that happened today.

But it was hard to do that. Vaughn had come inside me and despite the fact that he'd been just as shocked as I'd been, it didn't make me feel any better. I was beginning to regret ever starting this affair.

"You know, Sof," Jack was saying, "sometimes I feel as though I'm married to an angst-filled teenager."

"That would be statutory rape," I muttered before catching myself. "Oh, wait – we don't have sex."

Jack shot me a dark look. "Come off it."

I shrugged. "I don't really care anymore."

Jack pushed his plate away and rose to his feet. "Let's go. Now."

"Go? Go where?" I was genuinely confused.

"Upstairs. To the bedroom. Let's make love until our eyeballs pop." There was an undertone of anger in his voice.

I simply stared at him, sizing him up – the neatly-pressed golf shirt, the parting of his thinning hair, the quiet anger in his chocolate-brown eyes... The thought of "making love" to my husband was making me physically sick. What was wrong with me?

"Don't be silly, Jack," I mumbled, regretting ever bringing up the subject. I regretted goading him into this.

"Sofia, I said let's go."

I threw a glare at him. "I'm not in the mood, Jack, and I haven't finished my supper."

"I don't give a damn. You started this, now you'll finish it," he snarled, staring me down. "Do I have to drag you upstairs and undress you?"

A memory of the past flashed past my eyes and I shook my head. "No," I said. "You don't."

He knew he was hurting me.

He knew it and he enjoyed it.

The one thing I would not do was scream. Screaming made it last longer.

As Jack pumped into me savagely, I lay on my back and mentally counted the minutes down. Foreplay was something he knew nothing about, or couldn't be bothered with. He'd pushed me onto the bed, wrenched my dress off, and just gotten to it; pinching my breasts, biting my nipples, as if that would turn me on.

Sex with Jack – when he was angry about something – was a type of punishment. He enjoyed this sadistic dominance, enjoyed hurting me with his c0ck. It was as if he thought he was transferring all his fury to me via cum. Now, he gripped both my wrists over my head, squeezing so tightly I thought he'd cut the blood circulation. Finally, pushing deep inside me and nearly crushing me with his full weight, he climaxed in a series of spurts, grunting with each one. He pulled out shortly after, rolling onto his back and panting, shifting as far away from me as he could get on our bed.

I bruised easily and I just knew he'd marked me. Pain vibrated through my entire body, but at least I'd remained silent. That was something I could hold on to, something I could be proud of.

"I'm going to take a bath," Jack murmured after a while, getting up.

I didn't bother to do anything. Instead, I turned my back to him and squeezed my eyes shut.

"What're you still doing in bed?" Vaughn asked from the bathroom. I could hear him opening the shower door, probably getting ready to go inside and install the piping.

He'd been here exactly twelve minutes.

"Sofia?"

Jack had hurt me more than he even cared to know. He never apologised when he got like this and I never expected it. If a rough fúck every few months was all he wanted from me, I could at least be thankful it wasn't a daily occurrence. And I could be doubly grateful that he was out the door at four this morning to rush to some client's aid in the city.

Every part of my body ached, including my head, which had decided to join the party.

I just couldn't get out of bed. Holly had been in to offer breakfast, which I'd politely declined. I felt like sleeping my life away and maybe that was what I would do.

"Are you sick?"

Vaughn was suddenly at my bedside, kneeling until we were eye-level. I pulled the comforter over my head.

Why can't he just fúck off?

"Poor Sofia," he said softly, gently pulling the comforter off my head and tucking it under my chin. He leaned in and pecked my cheek. "Can I get you anything?"

"Just go away."

He arched one brow. "No."

"If you're expecting sex, I'm sorry. Not today. The machine's broken," I muttered spitefully.

Vaughn's brow furrowed in confusion. "Expecting sex? I don't expect it, Sofia. In fact, I just like being around you."

I pulled myself into a seating position, leaning against the headboard. The covers fell to my waist. And I didn't care. I didn't care, damn it. Because he could look and see for himself what Sofia Harrington was really all about.

I saw Vaughn's eyes zone in on the crimson bruises on my breasts and didn't bother to cover myself up, despite how I could feel a blush on my face.

"What happened there?" he asked quietly, still kneeling on the carpet. His hand was on my thigh.

God, I was not going to cry. "None of your business. Will you just finish the shower and get the hell out of my life?"

"Is that his idea of foreplay?" he asked through clenched teeth, and without warning, he ripped the sheets off the bed, exposing my nudity. His eyes raked my body. "The cunt. The bloody cunt," he spat, gently touching the red flesh of my pelvis.

"Stop," I breathed. "Just stop."

"Does he do this all the time?"

"Why do you care?"

"Because you don't deserve this." Vaughn sat on the edge of the bed, his back to me. "You're beautiful, smart, funny, sexy –"

"You say all the right things, Vaughn. It's almost as if you mean them."

He turned to look at me. "I do mean them! I mean every single word that comes out of my mouth!"

"You're not my husband and you're not my boyfriend!" I exclaimed, head pounding. "You're not even a fúcking friend. You're just... You're my toy boy and that's it. I don't need you to be my shoulder to cry on."

He was silent, his nostrils flaring. Then, "Do you love him?"

"I said, this is none of your business, Vaughn!"

He glared at me. "You should leave your husband. You're not happy. Yet you choose to stay. Is it for his money?"

I reached out and slapped him across the cheek, my arm regretting it. It was still sore from the night before.

But oh, it was worth it.

"You know nothing about me," I said through clenched teeth. "So shut the hell up and leave me alone."

"You're right. I should leave you alone." He stood up, his cheek still flaming red from where my hand had thwacked it. "Someone else will finish up your shower."

"Good."

"Good." He turned to leave. "You know, Sofia," he said quietly, standing in the doorway, "I might just be your twenty-seven-year-old boy toy but I've got more sense than you do."

I watched him leave.

And then I cried like I'd never cried before.

Chapter 8

His name was Richard and he finished the shower in one day.

Tall, bald and in his early fifties, he was both efficient and quiet, barely even grunting out a hello in my direction. Jack apparently knew him and they had a few drinks in the dining room when he was done.

"I just can't understand what was taking young Parker so long." Jack made the flippant comment to the older man.

"Beats me," Richard replied as Jack patted him on the back.

I retreated to my room and cried.

I was thirty-eight, for God's sake. Thirty-eight. Vaughn was about eleven years my junior, which meant that when I was starting high school, he was just saying his first word. Why on earth am I crying over him?

It just didn't make any sense.

When I finally crept downstairs, puffy-eyed and gloomy, I discovered that Richard had left and Jack was taking a dip in the pool. Holly was in the kitchen, making an early dinner.

"Are you ill?" she asked, concern filling her voice.

I certainly looked like hell. "I'm fine. Just a runny nose, I think."

"Oh, then you must stay in bed, Mrs. Harrington," she chided like a mother hen, ushering me out the kitchen. "I'll bring you a nice cup of lemon tea."

Feeling like a child, I listened to her and returned to bed, pulling the covers over my head.

You are being stupid, Sofia, my conscience scolded, wagging her manicured finger. Utterly and completely stupid. Are you really bawling over a boy toy that's jilted you?

Maybe that wasn't the reason I was crying. Maybe it was because I'd had a taste of freedom and hadn't wanted it to come to an end. Maybe it was because Vaughn made me feel human and showed me that there was more to life than...well, than being me.

But it had been stupid of me to begin the affair in the first place.

"Home, sweet home," Jack proclaimed, depositing his bags on the floor of our bedroom.

"Finally," I sighed, flopping back onto our bed, kicking my legs in the air. The road trip back home had been hell.

"Still feeling sick?" Jack managed a little concern in his tone as he looked down at me.

"No, I'm great," I said, forcing myself to sound like it. I started to remove the straps of my dress and gave him a seductive look. "Why don't you come here?"

"Now, Sofia?" he said reluctantly, but I could see the bulge in his trousers.

"Yes, Jack." I pulled him down on top of me and tried to stifle the brief moment of disgust at what I was doing.

But this time, he was gentle. Jack was a gentle person – when he wasn't angry. The only real problem I had was that when we ever had sex, his only concern was himself. He never cared whether I climaxed or not, as long as he did. Lying on top of me and thrusting inside, I felt his entire body stiffen and then relax as he spilled himself inside of me, his groans escaping into the air.

Sex was supposed to bring you closer to a person but I just felt empty and lonely inside.

The days following our return back to our little town of Northgate were filled with nothing for me. Jack went back to work, a little more tan than before, while I returned to my shopping and mindless chatter with my best friend, Daniella.

Daniella Townsend had been my best friend since secondary school, regardless of us being polar opposites. She'd always been the wild card, the girl who slept around, the girl with purple hair.

And now she was married with two kids and was chief of medicine at Northgate Memorial. To say she had it all would be an understatement.

"You look different. Something's different," she said as she hugged me, her familiar New Jersey twang music to my ears. Despite leaving New Jersey when she was eight, she'd clung to her accent like a lifebuoy.

"I got a tan?" I said, releasing her and gesturing at the grey sky. The sunny Comptons and dreary Northgate were literally worlds apart. "I certainly didn't miss this bleakness."

Daniella rubbed her hands together, obviously wishing she'd worn her gloves. "Yeah, rub it in, why don't you. No. I mean, you look...depressed."

"Why would I be depressed?" I asked, linking arms with her as we headed out of the cold and into the warmth of Starbucks.

"You tell me, Sofia. You tell me."

I didn't meet her eye. "I'm as happy as a bug. How's Nicholas?" I asked, referring to her husband. A smile crept onto my face at the thought of dear old blue-eyed Nick, Dani's college sweetheart. Not for the first time I wondered what it would be like to marry someone I'd known for so long, someone who worshipped at my altar.

"Nick's OK," Dani told me, "but I'm more worried about you."

"And Jess and Nico?"

"My kids are fine. Sof, stop skirting around this issue like a ratchet hoe on coke. Did Jack...hurt you?"

Daniella was very familiar with Jack's unpredictable temper. The first time he'd hurt me during sex, I'd gone running to her to ask if that was normal. She had been very emphatic when she'd told me that no, honey, it is not fúcking normal to want to bruise you in awkward places.

"You worry too much, Dan. Let's order."

"Because I love you. Because I know how much –"

"I had an affair, OK?" I interjected, just because she was getting so annoying. And also, I wanted to tell someone, wanted to rip the bandage off my just-healing wound.

"You what?" Dani's eyebrows had now relocated to her hairline. "Sofia! Who was it? When?" she hissed, grabbing my arm.

With someone I should never have even looked at, I thought wistfully.

"It's over, OK? Never screw a hillbilly. Lesson learned and all that."

"The Comptons is hardly a hick town. It's country. Stop being such a snob," she muttered, rolling her eyes. She paused to order two skinny lattes.

"He was just a boy."

Her eyes popped. "Like a college kid?"

"Close," I mumbled. "Almost thirty."

"Oh, wow. So...this affair...Was it worth it?" she asked me.

I bit my bottom lip. "I don't know."

"Feel guilty?"

"Of course. I wouldn't be me if I didn't."

"Still want the guy?"

Daniella knew the right questions to ask. I suddenly felt like our roles were reversed. She was cool, calm and collected Sofia, and I was wild, wacky and warped Dani.

"No, I don't. If you want to make me feel even guiltier, don't bother. I've already done that to myself," I said calmly.

"I don't want to make you feel guilty, Sof. I just want to find out why you're so sad."

I was watching porn.

My life was officially the thing underneath people's shoes that they scraped off against pavements. Jack had a business dinner with some big-shot client with a fat wallet, and Holly had retreated to her cottage for the night, leaving me to wallow in the main house for the night.

I knew that Jack's business dinners could last the entire night, and it had just struck seven p.m. Dani had a whole family to look after and wasn't available for a quiet night in, even if she did want to dissect my brief affair.

Therefore I was forced to watch a porno called True Cum. Cookie Ass-House was blonde, busty, had an annoyingly fake Southern twang, and could telepathically tell when a man was horny for her. She screwed guys in the diner she worked at, which was about the only thing this bad porno had going for it: The sex was good, the acting bad.

"I can tell..." Cookie wailed, as a potbellied vampire took her from behind "...that you are ...gonna come!"

That was my cue to turn off the TV and once I did, I found that that piece of awful acting had left me horny. I never watched blue movies but they always seemed to fascinate me. What would it be like, to be so comfortable with your body that you could fúck on cue in front of a dozen spectators? To put every inch of your body – especially your most intimate parts – on display for the world to perve over?

Stomping upstairs, thoughts of Vaughn invaded my mind.

What's he doing right now? Who's he doing right now?

Depression set in when I couldn't find my dildo. Knowing Jack, he'd probably thrown it out. I'd had to replace it five times already and they knew me by name at the sex shop.

"It's embarrassing," he'd said furiously, "for my wife to own sex toys. What does that say about our sex life?"

That it's worse than Oprah's, I thought, now mad myself.

Jack was a control freak and I was the wimp that let him be that way. He was never going to change and I was beginning to get sick of trying to change him. Vaughn thought I was staying with him for his money and maybe...maybe he was right. But Jack was the only family I had now. Without him, I'd be alone.

I ended up falling to the bed, squeezing my eyes shut. Sleep wouldn't come.

"I had no idea Gunter worked in the city," I mumbled, shoving a stick of gum into my mouth and staring up at the man's Kensington mansion. It was double our house and, for a single man, far too big. The cold night air bit at my skin and I pulled my shawl a little tighter around my shoulders.

Jack frowned down at me, handing the car keys to the young valet. "Do you really want to be chomping like a horse?"

I shrugged. "I don't know."

"This isn't a birthday party; this is business," Jack said passionately. "I don't want my wife coming off cheap in front of everyone, so spit that gum out."

I threw him a glare but obliged. Someone un-lucky was going to have strawberry gum under their expensive shoes. "I won't embarrass you, Jack. I swear."

"Good." He straightened his tie and took my arm, all but dragging me to the front door. "If I become his lawyer...well, let's just say I'll be able to wipe my ass with hundreds."

"Yippee."

"Good evening," the man at the door said jovially, an official-looking clipboard in hand. "Names please?"

"Mr. and Mrs. Harrington," Jack said clearly. I knew he got a special thrill from being on anybody's list.

The man skimmed down the A4 before nodding. "Ah, yes. Please, come in."

I found it ridiculous to have such a hullabaloo over a simple dinner. Jack's friends were stupidly ostentatious to say the least, especially Gunter van der Venter. Dressed in a ridiculous, silvery tuxedo and black top hat, he looked like a circus master.

"The gorgeous Mrs. Harrington," he said, smooching my cheeks. "I hope Jack is treating you well?"

Jack forced a laugh. "Of course I am."

Liar, I thought bitterly, pasting a smile on my face. No one would be able to tell how miserable I was.

"He is," I assured Gunter.

"Good. Mingle with the other guests, please. I always enjoy a little fun before the actual dinner. It works my appetite up," Gunter continued, gesturing at the fancy-dressed people swarming his large entertainment room. "May I just steal your husband for two seconds?"

Steal him for the rest of my life, I thought.

"Of course," I said aloud.

I watched them go, heads bent in animated discussion. Now I was free to find the bar. I was sure a wealthy German man like Gunter had a well-stocked bar. Pushing through the sea of laughing people, I finally found it – a small room beside the entertainment one with a counter on one side and a bartender standing behind it, an array of liquor on the shelves behind him. The room was already crowded with people that had the same idea as me but I made sure I pushed myself to the front.

"Your best wine," I told the bartender, breathing a sigh of relief when he set the glass down before me minutes later.

I downed it in one swig and left the bar. Jack was lost in the deluge of people and I didn't even care. In fact, I wished I could sneak out and just go home. But Jack would slaughter me if I wangled the keys from the valet and left him stranded, and I didn't feel like calling a taxi at night. So I would drink myself into a stupor and maybe the emptiness I felt inside would diminish slightly.

It had been such a shit idea to go and fúck someone who treated me fantastically.

"Sophie?" someone called from behind me.

I spun around, nearly tripping over my own heels, and came face to face with Harriet bloody Periwinkle. "It-it's Sofia."

"Oh right!" She smacked her forehead. "You look...lovely."

I glanced down at the white Grecian dress I'd casually thrown on. The dress had actually met Jack's approval. "Thank you. You too."

It was a lie. Her brown floor-length pen-cil-skirt dress was hideous. Back in the Comp-tons, she'd looked so put together. I started to wonder if maybe she had a controlling husband. Maybe he wanted her to look awful so she wouldn't attract any attention from any men. Or women.

"Is Jack here?" she asked lightly, dragging me from my own head.

"Yes. And your husband?" I certainly wasn't going to embarrass myself by attempting to remember his name.

"Mingling," she replied. She gave me a con-spiratorial grin. "I guess it's just us girls now."

"Er...I have to go...check on my hair."

"Oh, I'll come with you. I know where the loo is."

"I mean, my pubes," I muttered, turning on my heel and practically dashing through the crowd.

I headed out into the hallway, breathing deeply. Harriet was obviously a closet lesbian. Or just bisexual. Either way, I wasn't interested. There was only one other person I was interest-ed in and he wanted nothing to do with me. It was for the best.

"A bit stuffy in there, isn't it?" a voice came from somewhere in the hallway.

I just couldn't catch a break, could I? I didn't want to "mingle" or "have fun before eating". I wanted to be left alone but Gunter's guests were clearly a sociable bunch. So I turned to tell whoever-it-was that I wasn't in the mood for small talk.

The words died on my lips.

"Vaughn?" I sputtered, staring at the tall hulk of a man in a charcoal-black suit. His hair was combed back, neater than I'd ever seen it, and his eyes were an electric green. They were widened in disbelief.

"Sofia?" He came a bit closer, eyes narrowing. "What the hell are you doing here?"

"My...husband is friends with Gunter. What are you doing here?"

"I work at van der Venter Inc.," he said nonchalantly, referring to Gunter's software company.

"But...you're a plumber," I breathed.

"No, I'm a software designer," he said slowly, as if he was talking to a small child. "Chief software designer, actually. I was on vacation, just like you, but I wanted to help my father out. I was supposed to go into the family business once upon a time."

I swallowed. "Why didn't you tell me?"

He lifted a shoulder. "You never asked."

I gazed up at him, taking in those familiar green eyes, the onyx curl that had just escaped whatever gel he'd used to keep his hair neat. The familiar pull in my abdomen was still there, still intense. I ached to have his arms around me, to have him groan my name the way he did...

"Well, I have to go," he was saying, jerking a thumb at the entrance to the entertainment room. "My date's waiting for me."

"Of...of course," I said, licking my lips. My mouth had suddenly gone dry and my chest constricted. A date. Possibly his age or younger, with legs like skyscrapers and a waist like a violin. Damn it. Jealousy put a bitter taste in my mouth.

Vaughn looked skyward, muttering to himself. His gaze swung back to me.

"I didn't think I'd ever see you again," he said quietly.

"Me neither."

"You look...good."

I clung onto that simple compliment like a dog with a bone. "Thank you."

"You need to get back in there, Sofia. Your husband."

I nodded. "Yes. Unfortu-"

Vaughn's mouth cut me off. Falling back into the pattern, I looped my arms around his neck and pressed myself against him as hard as I could, amazed to feel the promise of his erection pressing back.

"I've missed you," I said into his mouth, not caring how desperate I sounded. I was desperate; desperate for him, for what he gave me and made me feel.

"You have no idea, Sofia," he murmured back, gripping my ass in his hands. "Gunter has ten bedrooms. Pick one."

"I don't care. Take me. Please, Vaughn."

He released me, snapping his head back to appraise me. "Follow me upstairs."

"Yes. Oh God, yes."

For this blissful moment, I could pretend I was single. But you know what they say about bliss.

CHAPTER 9

My dress was the first thing to go. Vaughn worked out how to get it off, and the cloud of fabric pooled at my feet, rendering me utterly and completely bare. I pulled his jacket off and undid his tie while his hands roamed all over me, as if he needed to remind himself of what I felt like. The anticipation of this man inside me was far too great my hands were shaking.

Vaughn picked me up and carried me to the opulent king-sized bed, simultaneously unzipping himself. Wrapping my arms around his neck, we fell together, the bed catching us.

Gunter certainly knew how to choose a bed, I gave him that.

"Do you think we can skip dinner?" Vaughn breathed into my neck, nipping at the soft skin there.

"Definitely." I released a low moan when he slipped a thick finger inside me. He slipped in another, finding my most sensitive part in an instant, his thumb massaging my clít. Any touch was a good touch and, arching my back, I came into his hand, gasping for air.

"Holy shit, that was quick," he remarked, eyes burning into mine. He withdrew his fingers, putting them to his lips and tasting. "You're so responsive, Sofia. It never gets old."

Heat burned my skin. "I want you. Please. Now."

"I want you, too. So, so much."

"Then fúck me."

"Commanding." Sliding over me, he pressed his mouth against mine and I could taste the saltiness of my own arousal. He pulled back, eyes glazing. "I like it."

And he punctuated his sentence by entering me swiftly, as hard as an electricity pole. I let out a gasp of surprise, my body trying to remember what it felt like to be stretched like this, beore I gripped him even tighter and wound my legs around his waist.

Vaughn's mouth was everywhere – on my neck, on my nipples, on my mouth... I let him taste my skin, absorb my scent. His hips jerked, pushing his c0ck deep into me, his deep thrusts turning me inside out. The scent of what we were doing was in the air, invading my nostrils, reminding me of our time back in the Comptons.

It was too much for me. Scraping my nails down his back and clenching my inner muscles, I came again, tears prickling my eyes.

"So beautiful," he groaned, resting his forehead against mine. "Gonna come, sweetheart."

He exploded inside me seconds later, his harsh breath ghosting over my lips.

"Sofia..." he whispered, still catching his breath. My eyes shut. "I can't be mad at you for staying with him."

I was instantly taken back to the mini argument we'd had the day he'd left me. I hated the memory. Hated the things I'd said, the things I'd felt.

"Let's not talk about him," I whispered back, biting his bottom lip.

Vaughn flipped me over, spearing me with his cóck. "Sofia, I can't not talk about that prick." He thrust upwards, gripping my waist.

I let out a squeal of surprise. The man was voracious. "It's hardly a turn-on," I said, catching my breath and placing my hands on his chest. I suddenly wished he were as naked as I was.

Vaughn slapped my ass. "Then what does turn you on?"

"You," I replied boldly, leaning forward. He inhaled sharply. "You are my sexy…" I clenched my cúnt around him "…little…" I ran my tongue across his chest "…boy toy…" I shifted slightly, milking him as tightly as I possibly could "…and you turn me on like a fúcking sprinkler."

Vaughn squeezed his eyes shut. "Why are you so sexy?" he growled, opening them again. I stared down into them, my breath tickling his face.

"You mean for an old hag?"

His palm smacked my butt cheek once more and he groaned at the resultant squeeze around his length. "You're not an old hag. You're a gorgeous older woman."

My heart was running a race. "Vaughn, I'm scared that this is more than sex."

His brow furrowed. "Do you want it to be more than sex?"

"I'm married," I said in a small voice. "It can't be."

"He's a dick, Sofia. I've never even met the guy and I can't fúcking stand him."

He sounded so vehement I was momentarily taken aback. "He has his moments. I... I loved him once. He's all I have."

"You have me."

Oh, sure. We also have eleven years between us.

"This is just sex. Good sex. The best sex," I whispered, feeling him lengthen inside me.

He gave me a strange look. "You're right. Let's not talk about him."

Jack was the last thing on my mind when Vaughn began his slow, upward thrusts. It was always different when we were on a bed. More intimate. More dangerous. And just when I didn't think I could come again, Vaughn reached up and pinched my nipples and I was consumed by my orgásm.

Exhausted, I fell on top of the man that had ruined me for my husband, shivering when he pecked my cheek before rolling me over and pulling out. I hadn't even noticed that he'd put a condom on until just then. Watching him stride into the bathroom, I didn't want to think about having him inside me with nothing between us again. He'd brought a date and I was married.

The stupid part of me relished what it felt like to feel him slip under the covers beside me, pulling me into his hard chest. Despite how wrong it was, I snuggled into him, grateful for his warmth.

"Are we cuddling now?" he asked after a long moment of heavy breathing had passed.

"It definitely feels like it," I whispered. It had been so long since I'd felt this safe, this cherished.

"We shouldn't."

He was right. Of course, he was right. "Okay." I began to pull away from him. He pulled me back.

"That doesn't mean we can't," he said softly, teasing his hands through my hair. "Look at us – fúcking in Gunter van der Venter's guest room. We're evil."

I laughed softly. "With my husband downstairs." The laughter died on my lips. With my husband downstairs.

On Gunter's boat, he'd been upstairs.

"We're going straight to hell." Vaughn pressed his mouth against my exposed neck. "I want you again," he breathed, his hand cupping one of my breasts.

"Vaughn...we can't. We have to go." I didn't sound convincing to my own ears.

"If you say so." His tongue was on my skin, licking its way around to my earlobe. "You still say so?"

The door swung open and a weird sense of déjà vu washed over me. Instinct told me to delve under the covers and I did, thinking to myself, I'll be damned if that's Harriet Periwinkle again!

"You said she's downstairs?" European accent. Male.

"That's where I left her. She does what she's told." British. Male. So, so familiar.

"We can have a quickie. A very quick quickie. No one will look for us here. Now kiss me." Muffled moans.

"You fúckshit!" Vaughn growled from beside me, tensing. I felt him sit up, felt him slide out the bed.

"Vaughn?" Now I recognised the voice as Gunter's.

"Er...Parker?" This voice... This voice I knew very well.

Pushing the covers off me, I sat up.

And stared at Gunter and Jack, who were still holding hands.

I flung an ice pack at him, mentally laughing manically when it hit him square in the face.

"What the hell's wrong with you?" Jack murmured, his hands flying to his already crimson face.

"You're what's wrong with me," I spat, folding my arms across my chest.

Jack gave me a pitiful look, resting one elbow on the kitchen counter. "I have every right to press charges against that –"

"Against my fúck buddy?"

Jack's face became stone. "He assaulted me. I am within my rights to press charges."

"No, you're within your rights to shove your díck up Gunter's ass," I barked. "But oh, wait, you already do that!"

"Just where do you get off being so high-and-mighty, Sofia?" Jack stood a little straighter. "You were screwing the plumber! He's a kid!"

"Yes, he is. Maybe we can share him, though I suppose you like your men like fine wine – ancient," I said through clenched teeth. I reached out and slapped his shoulder.

Jack had the grace to blush, rubbing where I'd hit him. "Don't act so pious. You were cheating on me!"

This was surreal. "There's no excuse for what I've done but Jack, the guy's overweight, balding and clearly a pússy. I mean, aren't gay people supposed to have taste?"

"I'm not gay." Jack's voice was loud and furious. He grabbed me by the shoulders, pushing his face into mine. Suddenly, a snake of fear crept down my spine and all the audacity the wine had given me dissipated.

"You are a whore. A slut," Jack said in a low baritone. "I picked you up off the streets, Sofia, and I can easily toss you back there. Don't you ever forget that, you ungrateful little wench." His fingers bit into my shoulder blades. "And don't you dare go running off to that Italian prostitute best friend of yours, screaming blue murder."

He nodded when my eyes widened. "Oh yes, her dumb as a lamppost husband confronted me the first time I disciplined you, can you imagine? How dare you embarrass me like that?"

"Jack! You're...hurting...me!"

His brow creased. "Am I? Oh, sorry." And he ended his apology by effortlessly shoving me across the kitchen.

Disbelief mingled with panic and, with no way of stopping my imminent fall, I tumbled and hit the refrigerator head first, my skull ringing.

"If I ever hear one word about...about Gunter and me, Sofia – I will kill you," Jack said from somewhere above me, digging his toe in my gut for good measure. "And you know the funny thing? No one will miss you. Because you have no one. Only me, Sofia. Only me."

Somewhere outside, a bird was chirping. Birds never chirped in the city. Unless they were pigeons, and everyone knew pigeons were rats with wings.

I tried to sit up, gingerly placing a hand on the side of my head. Pain reverberated in every inch of my body.

Definitely swollen, I thought, grimacing. The bump on my head felt like a goose egg.

Jack must have taken me upstairs after I'd obviously passed out, which was a bitch move as there was the strong possibility that I was concussed. Then again, he obviously wasn't thinking straight now that his secret was out. Glancing around the room, I blinked a few times, shaking my head. This wasn't our bedroom.

"Jack?" I croaked before clearing my throat to try again. "Jack!"

Someone appeared in the doorway. Someone who wasn't my husband.

"You're up."

"Vaughn? Where...where am I?"

He had a tray of breakfast in hand. "My place." Setting it on my lap, he took a seat beside me. "I'm going to take you to the hospital in a little bit. You could be concussed."

The scent of bacon and egg wafted into my nostrils and my stomach growled.

"Are we still in Northgate? How...how did I get here?"

"Yeah," he replied, "and my Beemer, of course."

"You know what I mean," I said, spearing a bacon rind with my fork and shoving it down my throat. "Christ. This is heaven."

Vaughn patiently watched me ravage the plate, a small smile on his face. "I found you in the kitchen," he said quietly. "Your kitchen."

I met his eyes, reddening. "How'd you know where I live?"

"Because I followed you home," he admitted. "Sofia, even before I met the guy, I knew that he was manipulating you. You weren't happy – aren't happy. You don't deserve shít like that from anybody, least of all a man who's supposed to cherish you for the rest of your life."

I felt like crying. I could feel the surge of waterworks in my tear ducts, in my throat.

"What did you do to him?" I asked after a long while, breathing deeply. I knew that Jack wouldn't just have let Vaughn waltz into the house to take me away.

Vaughn looked me in the eye. "I beat the horseshit out of him, of course. He can consider that round two."

"Vaughn," I began in a panic, "he's going to run to the police. You'll be thrown in prison and I can't have –"

"No, he's not." He reached out and wiped an oil smear from the side of my mouth with his thumb. "And Gunter isn't firing me, either. Everything's going to be fine. You wanna take a shower?"

"Thank you."

"And then we're going to the hospital."

My eyes widened. "No."

"Yes."

"No."

"Yes," he said through clenched teeth. "He must've killed twenty brain cells braining you against the fridge. So we're gonna find a nice doctor to check your sexy head, okay? OK. Now go shower."

I blinked at him. "All right."

He took the tray and got up. "I'll be in the kitchen." And he left.

Falling back onto the pillows, I looked around me. I was in Vaughn's bedroom. I didn't need to ponder how intimate that was. Kicking the covers off, I got to my feet shakily, glancing down at the oversized Arsenal T-shirt I was wearing. Cute. I was Manchester.

The bathroom door was ajar, and once I took a good look at myself in the mirror, I could see that I desperately did need that shower. One side of my head was an angry red and my temple sported a purpling bruise. My hair was dry as hell, not to mention all over the place. And now I had bacon fat all over my face.

So pretty.

I wrenched the T-shirt off and shimmied out of my panties. Adjusting the temperature in the shower, I slipped into the stall, the water a balm to the aches all over my body. Squeezing my eyes shut, I began to contemplate my options.

I could divorce Jack. But then...where would that leave me? Thank God we'd never been stupid enough to have children.

I could always go back to work. Dani could help me out there. But where would I stay?

And Jack...In a weird way, I did care about him, despite everything, He'd been so sweet when we'd started dating... This monster wasn't the man I'd married.

"Are you okay?"

I whirled around, catching Vaughn's silhouette in the mottled glass of the shower door.

"Yeah. I'm fine," I lied.

"I'll be in the room. Take your time. Shout if you need me."

My tears were mingling with the water. "Vaughn?"

"Yeah?"

"Can you come in?"

The door opened a crack. "Babe." He pulled it open and stepped in, fully-clothed. "I'm sorry I wasn't there." He wrapped his arms around me, pulling me into an embrace.

I don't know how long we stood there under the water, but the hot water ran out and Vaughn scooped me up, elbowing the door open.

"You know you can stay here however long you want," he said gently, toweling me dry like a baby. "I don't mind in the slightest."

"I can't."

He stopped his ministrations. "Sofia. You know I love you, right?"

"No. No. No."

"I love you, I love you, I love you," he repeated, staring down into my eyes.

"And when did you realise that?" I asked him, staring somewhere else. "Was it the first or second week of my holiday with my gay husband?"

"I think it was when you offered me coffee." He pecked my forehead.

"Love doesn't happen that quickly," I informed him. Of course, he was too young to know this. The real world wasn't a soap opera. Case in point, my world.

"Who says?" he countered, watching me loop the towel around myself. "There's no formulaic

equation to love, Sofia. I know what I feel. Here."
He pressed his hand to his chest.

I swallowed. "I'm a married thirty-eight-year old."

"A soon-to-be single thirty-eight-year old." His eyes searched mine. "You're not going back to him, are you? You can't."

I took a deep breath, unable to make myself look him in the eye. "Vaughn...I've decided what I want to do," I said. "But I'll do it on my own."

Chapter 10

The two weeks I spent in Nick and Dani's spare bedroom passed in a blur and, surprisingly, they were two of the best weeks I'd had in a long time. Instead of feeling pathetic and sorry for myself, I took that time to regroup and reassess my life – or, more accurately, what was left of it.

The day after Jack had assaulted me, Dani and I took half an hour to pack what little was mine into boxes and bin bags once we'd found that the house was empty and the spare key was where I usually left it. As I'd suspected, Jack had gone to work like normal, and with a sinking feeling, I realized that it was normal for him to manipulate me like that; for him to hurt me like that.

That moment of realisation sent me over the edge and Dani had had to restrain me from trashing the house I'd never called him. I wasn't going to be a fucking martyr and "only take what I'd come into the marriage with". No, I took whatever the hell I wanted, imagining that I'd sell most of it, especially since a trip to the ATM had revealed that he'd frozen my account, leaving me penniless.

Out of everything, saying goodbye to Holly was the worst part. She was a friend, a mother and a confidante all these years and the idea of not seeing her again made me weepy.

"I'm glad, Sofia," she'd said, using my first name for the first time ever. After copping a look at the bruising I'd tried to hide, the smile on her face seemed forced. "I'm glad you're going away for good. Mr. Harrington just isn't husband material. He doesn't know how to do it."

"You…you know about that?" I'd sputtered, rubbing at my red eyes while Dani ferried boxes to her car.

Holly snatched my hands in hers, squeezing. "I have eyes, my dear, and I can see that you weren't happy," she said gently. "But this last holiday? Something changed over those two weeks. You were smiling more. Younger men will do that to you."

My eyes had widened, mortification that this older woman knew of my indiscretion setting in. "How did you –"

"The first time I visited my niece over there, she was actually sick," said Holly, "but after that? I reckoned you needed some time alone with your young man. So I kept going out."

I couldn't believe it.

"You deserve to smile," she went on. "Just so you know, dear, a man who can make you smile and forget your troubles, is a man worth keeping around." Then she told me that she was handing in her notice to Jack.

So I had nothing to my name but the few items I deemed important. Jack's lawyer had served me with divorce papers two days after Gunter's party and I briefly considered framing them before I remembered that they had to be signed and sent back. Once the divorce finally came through, I would be Sofia Lopez again and I could breathe.

But I had no Vaughn.

He'd stopped calling after a week of my ignoring him and stupidly, I felt his absence like a missing limb. He only wanted what was best for me. He'd said he loved me. Of course, it was probably in pity. Or maybe just a ploy to get me to leave Jack. Either way, loving someone because you pitied them wasn't love, no matter what he wanted to believe in his fabulous rainbow-filled dreamland. We hadn't known each other that long and, despite how much he made me laugh, we were all about sex. Great sex does not a relationship make.

"Penny for your thoughts?" Dani wanted to know, sliding a hot cup of tea across the table to me.

Sunlight streamed through the open windows and into the small dining room, setting the Sunday breakfast my best friend had made aglow. She sat across from me in a ratty terrycloth bathrobe, her strawberry-blonde hair tamed into a ponytail.

I shook my head, pushing all depressing thoughts of Vaughn aside. Reaching into the pocket of my nightgown, I pulled out a lone Pill and popping it into my mouth before chasing it with my tea. The black liquid burned going down my throat and I took a few seconds to offer Dani a lame, "I wasn't thinking."

Dani arched a brow. "Don't insult my intelligence, Sof. Come on. It's just us girls today."

Nick had taken Jess and Nico to his mother's place for the day and the house seemed so big and empty without fourteen-year-old Jess nattering on the phone and eleven-year-old Nico shooting things on his Xbox.

"Fine. I'm thinking about what the hell I'm going to do." My eyes shifted to the Classifieds I'd been meaning to check out after breakfast. Just the thought of paging through all these odd jobs at my age was enough to make the bacon in my gut want to re-emerge.

Danielle's face softened. "You know you can stay here as long as you like, sweetheart," she told me. "Nick likes you, my children adore you – way more than they like me, that's for sure – and I love coming home to catch up on Teen Wolf episodes with you."

"You know we're too old for that show, right?"

She waved a flippant hand. "Old, schmold. Jess thinks I'm cool. Totally worth it."

I laughed, and the sound was strange to my ears. "I can't stay with you and your family forever, Dan. I need to start fresh, get back out into the real world." I sighed. "Being with Jack was certainly living a sheltered lifestyle."

Danielle scowled. "Don't even mention that abusive twat's name in this house," she snarled.

"You're miles better off without him, Sof. Listen, the hospital might need –"

"No, thanks," I said quickly, gripping my cup a little too tightly. "I...I miss nursing, working with you, but this time, maybe I should do something different."

She gaped at me. "Like what?"

"I don't know." I bit my bottom lip. "I really don't know."

Dani beamed at me. "I have an idea you might actually like..."

Before I went to nursing school, I did some secretarial work and that was why Dani figured I'd be pregnant to as a temporary replacement for Nick's heavily pregnant secretary. Nick owned a garage that did custom jobs on cars and bikes. A week on the job and the most I'd done was to create a new, more efficient filing system for repair orders and the like. I was shocked by how many cars were involved in wreckages. Not being able to drive suddenly seemed like a blessing, as did submerging myself in the little intricacies of a repair shop.

But being alone in the front of the shop meant that my thoughts could hang above me like a dark cloud, just waiting for the chance to rain. Worries... Worries were like a plague of locusts. Was I ever going to get out my best friend's house, no matter how much she insisted I wasn't a burden? Was I ever going to be able to stand on my own two feet after so long of being carried by a husband who only wanted to control me?

Will I ever forget Vaughn bloody Parker?

That question haunted me every waking moment. During the day, when I was at the computer, wondering if he stared at his own screen and squinted at the rays like I did. And at night, when I was alone in bed, the memory of his thick c0ck inside me as clear as if it was yesterday. The nights were the worst for me. Sometimes, I cried. I never knew my tear ducts could produce so much liquid until I cried for Vaughn bloody Parker.

He'd stopped calling. I'd stopped pretending I didn't care.

I'd gone three weeks without sex. Maybe that was all I was missing when it came to Vaughn. Maybe that was the only reason I was going out of my mind missing him.

You should call him, the voice in my head said desperately.

But I couldn't call him. I could never go back to him. My mind kept replaying his declaration of love – his silly, out-of-the-blue declaration – and the more I thought of it, the more ridiculous I felt. How would the two of us work exactly? Me, with my struggle with independence, my open wounds from my disaster of a marriage. Him, utterly boyish and naïve and sexy-as-sin. I'd always be thinking of our eleven-year age gap, would probably constantly be out of my mind with jealousy whenever he so much as glanced at a younger girl.

No, I needed someone my own age; someone mature and on the same level as me. Someone who didn't claim to be in love after two bloody weeks of fúcking nonstop. Someone who didn't look like he'd just stepped out of a GQ. Someone who didn't say ridiculously sweet things to me when I was in his arms, or when he was inside me, or when…

"Stop it, Sofia," I said aloud, receiving a strange look from Jon, one of Nick's mechanics. He'd come to my desk to use the telephone.

"Yes, I talk to myself. What of it?"

Jon held his tattooed arms up, stepping away from my desk. "Nothing. As you were," he added before backing away.

"Do me a favour and man the phone line for me, Jon? Tell Nick I'm going out for lunch," I said to him, already gathering up my things. It was nippy outside, as it always was, and my coat was one of those big, thick and fleecy movie-star ones.

"Yeah, fine." He glanced at his grimy hands. "I'll just…hang around for a bit."

Shouldering my handbag, I stepped outside, rubbing my hands together. There was a McDonald's just a block away from the garage and the short walk gave me little time to think about how pathetic my life was. Getting a ride to my boss's house with my boss to sleep in my boss's guest room, just two doors away from my boss. Being so stupid to never think of putting some money away for myself during my ten-year marriage. Never standing up for myself whenever Jack would hit me. Never... The list was endless.

Stupid, stupid Sofia, all alone in this world.

But I wasn't alone, was I? I had Danielle. I had her family. I had Vaughn.

Yes – had him. Past tense. You don't have him anymore and you're better off, right?

The voice in my head was a bitch and I didn't want to listen to her anymore. She was still going off in my head when I finally joined the line in McDonald's and my mental argument with her was the sole reason I didn't notice Jack until he walked right up to me, a paper bag already in hand.

"Sofia?"

He'd shaved his hair, giving the illusion that he'd never had a receding line, and his murky brown eyes now blinked at me from behind wire-framed glasses. Despite the fact that this was a weekday, he was in a golf shirt and jeans – Jack thought denim was for hipsters – with loafers. My once-over ended when my eyes settled on his bare ring finger.

"Jack." Cold detachment was what I settled on. For weeks I'd wondered if I'd quiver at the sight of him again, or if I'd finally fly into a rage over the way he'd brutalised me over the years.

"I thought it was you," he said softly, audible even though the restaurant was filled to the brim with people. "You look well."

I didn't. I looked like several kinds of animal excrement. My eyes were permanently swollen from crying so fúcking much, the black dress I wore beneath my silly coat was ill-fitting because I hadn't been eating much and my hair was in desperate need of a wash.

Yet Jack was complimenting me.

For a moment I could only gape at him, wondering what alternate universe I'd stepped into. Shaking my head, I moved forward as the person in front of me did, and Jack moved, too. I could smell his familiar cologne and I thought about covering my nose, or simply turning away and forgoing my lunch.

"So...how does it feel, being Sofia Lopez again?" Jack was saying. When I didn't answer, he said in a rush, "Things ended horridly. You deserved so much more and I wasn't it. I've been trying to get the courage to call you, tell you how sorry I am but every time I punch your number in, I end up putting the phone down."

"What do you want from me?" My voice was quiet, unwavering. I couldn't look at him but at least I could talk.

"I apologise, Sofia. I am so, so sorry for everything," was his fervent response.

"You can't say it, can you?" I tried to swallow past the ball that had suddenly wedged itself in my throat. "What you did over the years? You can't say it."

"I hurt and humiliated you. It wasn't anything you did – you have to understand – it was all me." He paused, and I could feel him willing me to look at him – so I did. "I've known I was attracted to other men for years. Since university.

I tried to fight it, to pretend I was a something I wasn't. You were beautiful and naïve and I thought if I married you, no one would question my sexuality." His eyes were glassy and I was horrified to realise that he was on the verge of tears. Jack. Jack Harrington was going to cry in line at Mickey D's. "Then when we found out that I can't have children... I was leading a double life and I'm sorry you wasted a decade on me because of my selfishness."

The tears were welling now but they weren't sad or angry ones for what had happened or what I could have had. I felt...relieved, like a weight had been lifted off my chest – because I, Sofia Lopez, was having an epiphany in a crowded fast food restaurant.

I didn't want to waste another ten years of my life wondering and hoping and wishing. Jack had been in denial about who he loved...and so was I.

"I have to go," I burst out, startling Jack.

"But you haven't had your lunch, Sofia. I was hoping we could –"

"No," I said, shaking my head, "there's someone I have to talk to."

"Is it…young Parker?"

I had just given my place up in line and was already making my way towards the door. A blush crept up my neck. Young Parker. Jack just had to remind me of that, didn't he?

"Here, Sofia," he called, and I turned to look at him. He was holding his bag out for me. "You should eat something. I can see your cheekbones. You looked prettier with more meat on you."

Surprised laughter left my lips and I took the proffered olive branch. "Thanks, Jack. Have a nice life." We would never be best friends and I hoped I'd never bump into him again, but it was obvious that he'd changed – that we'd both changed.

He smiled back at me. "You, too. I really do want that for you, Sofia. I want you to be happy. You deserve it."

And maybe he did, but ten seconds after saying goodbye to him, I started feeling absolutely silly for just about hinting to my ex-husband that I was chasing after a younger man. Shoulders sagging, I shuffled back into the front room of the garage, peeking into the bag of what would have been Jack's lunch: A large Big Mac and chips. My mouth watered.

"Ah, there she is." Nick's voice cut through the thick cloud of fast food and desperation that was surrounding me.

I looked up, intent on issuing a sincere apology for taking an early lunch. The words died on my lips. My mouth went dry, my breathing shallow. I couldn't get my fingers to work, so my burger fell to the concrete ground, golden chips escaping from the bag.

I squeezed my eyes shut and opened them again. Not a hallucination brought on by hunger. Not a daydream in the office.

Nick was standing at my desk with Vaughn.

"Well...this is awkward," Nick was saying, after looking at the mess on the floor. He flushed, running his hands through his messy brown hair. "I, ah, know Vaughn, you see. He's friends with my baby brother. Dani doesn't know so... This is awkward."

Blood rushed through my eardrums. I could barely make out what he was saying.

"Um, we don't have any Michelin tyres in stock, Sofia, do we?" he went on, ignoring the fact that I'd just dropped my lunch and gone motionless. "Sixteen-inch ones, for Harleys? None of the guys can find any in the stockroom."

Tyres and bikes. Right. That was what he was all about. That was what I should've been all about. But under Vaughn's piercing stare, it was all I could do to tell myself how to breathe.

"I...I don't know," I croaked out, and the words barely made it out my dry mouth.

"Of course, of course." Nick glanced at Vaughn. "She's new. But you already know that. I mean, you've been coming here for ages." His gaze returned to me. "I can't understand the new filing system for the list of what we've already put an order for."

"I just...put them in order of dates."

Nick gave out an audible sigh. "Give me a minute, man?" he grunted at the boy-man I'd only been thinking about minutes before. "My glasses are somewhere in my office."

"Yeah, sure. I'll just wait here."

Nick met my eyes. "You don't mind being left alone with him?"

I shook my head and he turned and left. My stomach instantly turned over. Alone. I was alone with Vaughn. I took that long moment of silence to let my eyes devour him. It was like seeing him for the first time. His black hair was cropped short now, only making the hard angles of his face stand out. The black T-shirt he wore was tight across his chest, as were the jeans hugging his thick legs.

I want to lick the stubble on your face, bite into your lips, suck the part of your body I crave to have in my mouth again...

"This was a complete coincidence, Sofia."

There was my name coming out his mouth again, said in that particular way. I didn't want to react to him this way but I was. I wanted him so badly my pússy was clenching around air.

"My tyre burst a few days ago," Vaughn continued, approaching me in a few long strides. "I completely wiped out, went skidding for a couple metres." He held his right arm up. The skin there was still red and looked a bit like raw, ground beef. "One of my battle scars. I trust Nick's crew to take care of my bike."

The little nurse in me was horrified at how nasty the wound was and grabbed his wrist without thinking. "Did you get this checked out? Fucking hell, Vaughn, did you just put mercurochrome on it and call it a day?"

The corners of his lips tipped up as he stared down at me. "You want to kiss it better?"

"I... Stop it. Please." I released him, instantly missing the feel of his pulse in his wrist. It reminded me that he was here, that I wasn't dreaming him up.

"You've lost weight," he observed, looking me over. "I don't like it."

I felt a blush bloom in my cheeks but my mouth remained shut.

"Have you been thinking about me?" Vaughn's voice was soft, so soft it felt like a gentle caress to my ears.

I looked away. "Yes." Why lie and say I hadn't?

Vaughn's fingers came up under my chin, making me face him. "Is your pussý wet?"

I gulped, shaking my head. Lies, lies, lies...

"I don't believe you," he said, frowning. My hand was swallowed in his as he effortlessly dragged me past my desk and through the doorway that led to the parts of the shop where work on the vehicles got done.

Vaughn obviously knew his way around the place because he pulled me into a small office I knew Nick used to hide stuff he purchased on eBay. Danielle didn't understand that her husband could bid on anything Hulk Hogan so much as breathed on.

But all that nonsense flew out my mind the instant the door was slammed shut and Vaughn's lips crashed against mine.

My knees buckled. I lost the use of my limbs. All I could do was stand there and accept the sweep of his tongue across my lower lip, open my mouth and grant him entry. I didn't know if the low moan came from my mouth or his, but I knew whose thighs were clenched together, hoping to relieve the ache between them.

"I don't believe your sweet little pussý isn't wet for me, Sofia," Vaughn murmured, sliding his hands beneath my coat and wrenching it off. "Have you fúcked anyone since me?"

"No," I moaned, my breath catching when he pushed up the hem of my dress and I felt his fingers on the inside of my thigh.

"Have you touched yourself thinking about me?" He cupped my cúnt, his fingers teasing the small lace triangle encasing it.

"No," I whispered, because how could I do that when my best friend was two doors away from my bedroom and her children's rooms on either side of mine?

But Vaughn misunderstood. His fingers stilled. "Who've you been thinking of, then?" Jealousy swirled in the emerald pools of his eyes.

"I-I haven't touched myself."

A slow smile softened his face but did little to diminish the wolf that he was. "You must be soaking, then. Poor Sofia. You'll cut off your nose to spite your beautiful face."

Then he sank to his knees, tugging my thong down.

Before I could protest, he had his hands on the back of thighs, holding me in place as he pressed a soft kiss against my entrance. As embarrassing as it was, I nearly came from that. My hands were on his head, saying what I couldn't say and making him eat me.

"I know what you need," he breathed against my pink flesh. "You just have to say it."

I huffed out a breath, my entire being thrumming with excitement. But I couldn't tell him how much I wanted him, how much I'd missed him. I just couldn't.

"Sofia." Vaughn's breath ghosted across my swollen clítoris.

I whimpered. "I...need...you. God, please, Vaughn. Make me come. Please, make me come."

I could feel him smile against my opening and then the only thing I could feel was the point of his tongue, licking its way up my slit. I threw my head back, biting my bottom lip so hard I instantly tasted metal. My clít was sucked past his lips like a tiny juicy fruit. Pleasure radiated from my very core and when Vaughn slid a finger inside me, fúcking it into me along with his tongue, I surrendered to it. I let myself be washed away with the force of my Orgasm. It was quick, it was intense and I just about collapsed all over the man at my feet in gratitude.

He rose, holding me to him as he did, and his lips found mine once more. The taste of my own excitement was heady and addictive. Looping my arms around Vaughn's neck, I surrendered to him completely.

"Do you want me to fúck you, Sofia?" he groaned, pulling my sore lip into his mouth and sucking it better.

My fingernails dug into his nape and, feeling the promise of his erection against my belly, I lost the ability to breathe.

"I want to fúck you, sweetheart," Vaughn said for me, his hands cupping my butt. "Want to feel your cúnt around my cOck like a fist. Want to fill you with my cum. I've missed putting a shocked expression on your face every time you come, sweet Sofia."

"I need you, Vaughn," I finally admitted. "I need you so, so much."

He was fumbling with his belt now, trying to free himself as quickly as possible. I whimpered; hungry, desperate.

"Bend over that desk, Sofia."

It was a small desk, pushed to one side and piled high with Hogan memorabilia. I let Vaughn go and did as he asked, fighting to get my long-sleeved dress off and leaving on what was underneath.

Bent over a desk with my back to him and my butt in the air, I felt, rather than saw, Vaughn cop a look at me.

"You're wearing my T-shirt."

It was totally traitorous to the Red Devils but only for Vaughn would I wear an Arsenal shirt. When I'd put it on today, feeling stupidly sentimental, the idea that he'd see me in it never even crossed my mind.

I was breathing deeply as I felt him approach me. My brain scrambled for something to say, anything to make me any less pathetic than I already seemed.

"You'd love to make this all about mindless sex, wouldn't you?" Vaughn's voice was defeated when he finally spoke. "You'd love for me to shove my cóck in you then go on my merry way. You'd love to wait a few days – maybe just one – before you called me for a quick fúck in my car. Repeat cycle. Am I right, Sofia?"

I closed my eyes, hating the tears that threatened to make an appearance. "Will you just fúck me already?" I forced myself to say.

"Is it the age thing?" He went on as if I hadn't said anything. "Who gives two shíts, Sof? Our relationship would be just that – ours. Yours and mine. No one else's. You're the most beautiful thirty-eight-year-old woman I've ever laid eyes on and you're the only woman I want. Fúck what people say."

"Until I turn forty and you lay eyes on a beautiful twenty-year-old," I bit out, tugging the shirt down my back to give me a modicum of decency. "It might seem hip right now to have a cougar on your arm but we'd never work, Vaughn. You'd want kids and I'd be...I'd be an old prune whose womb has withered away and...and –"

"Shut up."

"Excuse me?" I straightened, spinning around to face him. Anger made my heart pound faster. "I'm raising a valid argument here and you're telling me to shut up?"

"You just gave me flimsy excuses not to be with me. I don't find them valid anything."

"You're so...so –"

"Immature?" He quirked a brow. "Why are you wearing my T-shirt?"

The change in subject threw me momentarily. "Because it reminds me of you," I answered without thinking. "You can take it back if you want," I added curtly.

He gave me a satisfied smile. "I don't want it back. I quite like it on you. Red is your colour." But he was probably referring to the blush on my face.

"Vaughn," I said softly, unable to resist touching his arm, "I don't want to want you. It's selfish of me."

He laced his fingers with mine, looking into my eyes. "If we have kids, we have kids. And if we don't, we don't."

You say that now... I thought to myself.

Vaughn brought his forward down against mine. "But for now, I just want to make love to you on this desk with Hulk Hogan's creepy face staring at us. Then, I want to take you out to lunch, since you lost yours at the door. That would be considered as a date. If I'm really lucky, maybe you'll come home with me because I kind of liked seeing you in my bed. But only if you want to."

I let out a sigh, simply revelling in his attention. A date. I wanted that. I just wanted to be around him. Jack was right (I never thought I'd say that) – I deserved to be happy. Vaughn made me happy and I was sick of pretending I didn't care about him. Maybe I'd even get over the "age thing", as he so eloquently put it, someday. Maybe.

"Sof? Say something," he implored me, pulling back, his face wary.

"I just remembered – Nick doesn't wear glasses."

It was Vaughn's turn to flush. "Yeah, he's not great at ad-libbing. He was supposed to have to take a call."

"Come here, you sly dog," I murmured, pulling him back to me. "Make love to me."

He kissed the top of my head. "I think we should wait until I get you to my bed."

To my chagrin, he was already zipping himself back up. "Are you kidding me?"

He looked sombre. "You really want to have sex with the guy from Thunder in Paradise watching us?"

Sometimes, Vaughn's boyishness was endearing, like now. As he took me into his arms, just holding me to him as if I were the most precious thing in the world to him, I realised that yes, I might be eleven years older than the man I was about to declare my love to, but older didn't make me any wiser. He seemed to have his shít figured out whereas I...I was just starting a new chapter in my life. The page was blank for the moment and the author wasn't sure if the ending would be a happy one but one thing was for sure: Vaughn was going to be the hero. Always.